DON'T MAKE ME DO SOMETHING WE'LL BOTH REGRET

INNOVATIVE PROSE SERIES

Highlighting fiction, creative nonfiction, and hybrid works by underrepresented and minority authors

SERIES EDITOR
KATIE JEAN SHINKLE

BOOKS IN THIS SERIES

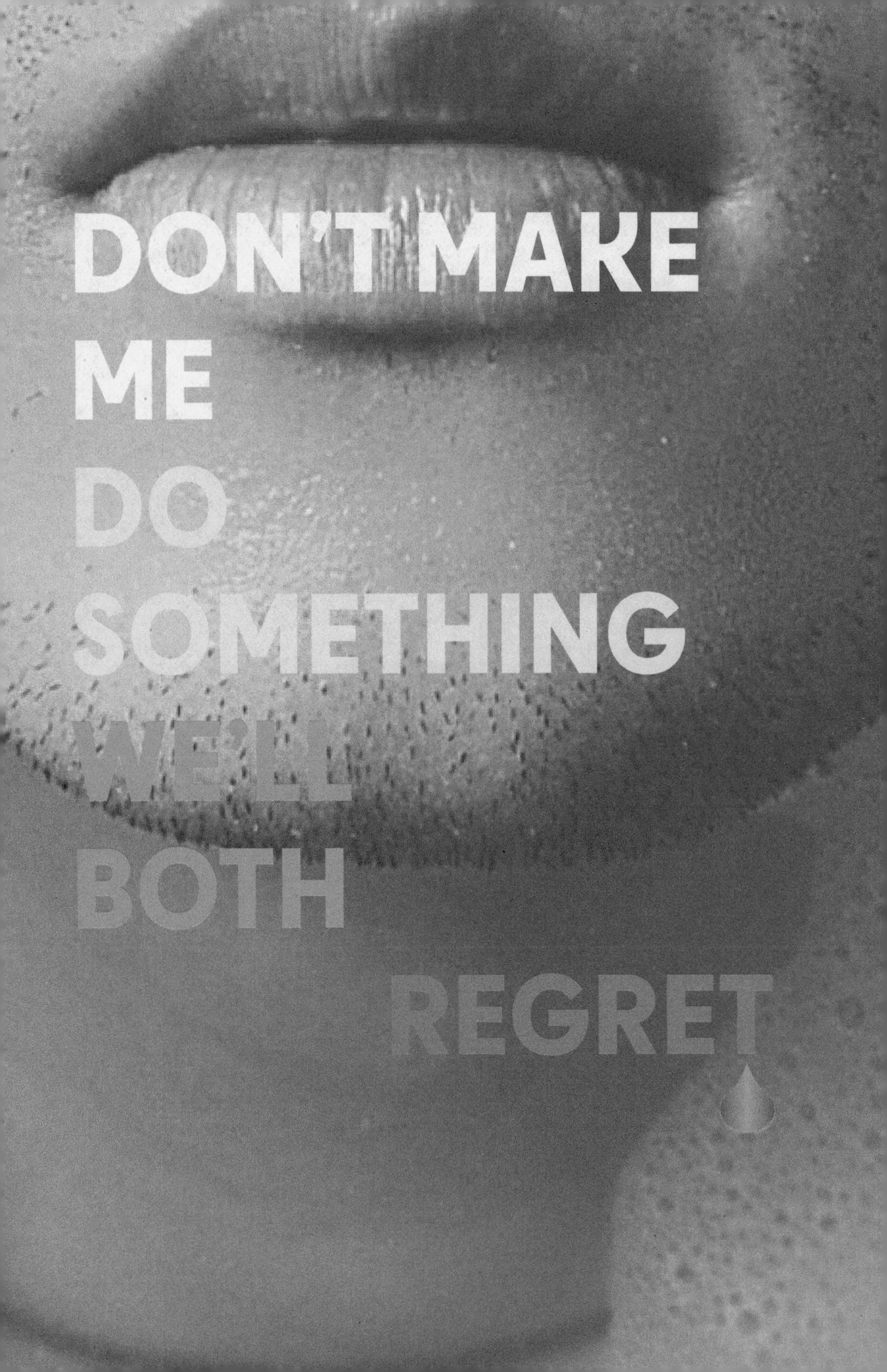
DON'T MAKE
ME
DO
SOMETHING
WE'LL
BOTH
REGRET

DON'T MAKE ME DO SOMETHING WE'LL BOTH REGRET

Tim Jones-Yelvington

★trp

The University Press of SHSU

Huntsville · Texas

www.texasreviewpress.org

Published by: TRP: The University Press of SHSU
Huntsville, Texas 77341
Library of Congress Cataloging-in-Publication Data.
Names: Jones-Yelvington, Tim, author.
Title: Don't make me do something we'll both regret : stories /
Tim Jones-Yelvington. | Other titles: Innovative prose.
Description: Huntsville, Texas : Texas Review Press, [2022]
Series:Innovative prose | Identifiers: LCCN 2021045679 (print)
LCCN 2021045680 (ebook) | ISBN 9781680032482 (paperback)
ISBN 9781680032499 (ebook) | Subjects: LCGFT: Short stories.
Gay fiction. | Classification: LCC PS3610.O637 D66 2022
(print)LCC PS3610.O637 | (ebook) | DDC 813/.6—dc23
LC record available at https://lccn.loc.gov/2021045679
LC ebook record available at https://lccn.loc.gov/2021045680
Photo fragments adapted/remixed for cover design: Hisu Lee_
unsplash.com, and Peter Paul Rubens: The Sacrifice of Isaac, Public
Domain, https://creativecommons.org/licenses/by -sa/4.0/deed.en.
Cover & Book design: PJ Carlisle
texasreviewpress.org

★trp

"I dream of being evil . . . an evil glamour that doesn't make us beautiful but that changes what beauty is."

—*Derek McCormack*

Contents

xi

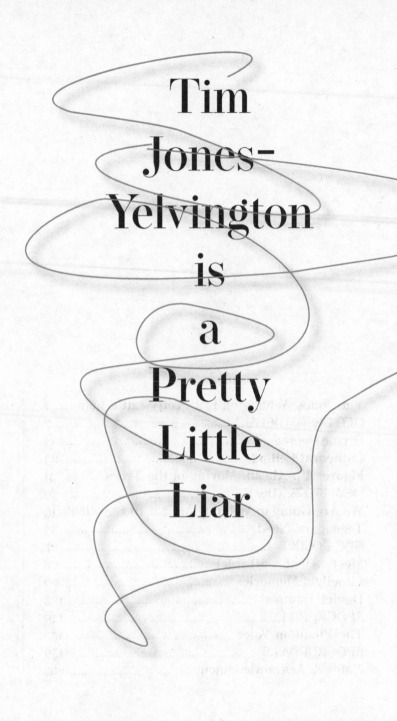

Tim Jones-Yelvington is a Pretty Little Liar

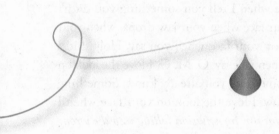

This is the new me: a well-appointed corpse. Jungle red lips, ironed locks, my power pant suit with the padded shoulders; lay me formidable in the grave. My gaggle flocks the coffin, they are crying. Mascara runs. Remember, my lovelies, the night we hopped our frienemy's fence? How we peeked through our frienemy's windows, how we witnessed SCANDAL, how we gasped and giggled and ran away?

This is a good look for you, our frienemy tells me, when the clergyman's back is turned. She spits, her saliva snakes through my foundation, exposes the skin that awaits decay. From beyond death's grip, I lower my voice, I beg her, under my breath, *Can we please not do this here?*

My lovelies, I haven't forgotten your secrets. Everything each of you told me in confidence. You said, Promise you'll keep this to yourself. You said, Promise you'll never tell a soul. You said, If anyone finds out, my life is over! I said, *I'll take it to the grave.* Once, I came upon our frienemy in the marketplace. *I know what you've been up to! Don't pretend your hemline's clean!* And she begged me, Keep your voice down. Don't make me do something we'll both regret.

This is the *new* new me. Black feathered collar, black feathered cuffs, gold-threaded jacket, my shoulder plumage spills. I am a peacock. My chin is cocked. I am a libertine. I am a dandy. I am an emu, ready to stretch my neck. To sharpen my beak. To peck out your eyes.

They say that she who holds the information flips the lever. I love the look on your face when I tell you something you didn't know. I love the look on your face when your jaw drops, when your eyes widen. I love the look on your face when you say, Holy shit! I love the look on your face when you say, O. M. G. I love the look on your face when I tell you something, you already know. Something only you could possibly know. I love the look on your face when I say, *Darling, we wouldn't want this information falling into the wrong hands, now would we?* I love the look on your face when you gasp, How did you know? I love the look on your face when you say, I've never told a soul! I love your look when I say, *I'll keep your secret, but there's something I need you to do for me. My lovely, you wouldn't want me to tell the others, now would you? My lovely, but don't they deserve to know? How can you expect me to keep this from them, my gaggle? Something like this?* My lovelies, I love the looks on your faces when I flip the lever. I love the looks on your faces when you're under both my thumbs. *I have a task for you, my lovelies. My lovelies, I'll never let you go. My lovelies, friendship is forever.* If you could only see the looks on your faces. Right. Now.

This is the *new* new new me. I bought a fascinator on Etsy. I bought these pigments at MAC. I bought these heels at that drag queen store in Boystown. I bought a Barbie on Ebay and I glued it to a hat. Certainly you must appreciate my pillbox.

They say that she who writes the text holds the power. Get it in writing, is what they say. *I wrote down your secrets, each and every one.* Recorded for posterity. I typed your secrets on my laptop and I tweeted them. I tweeted them with my private twitter, viewable only be me. Then I printed each tweet on fortune cookie paper. *I rolled up your secret fortune-tweets and tucked them in a locket.* This locket was shaped like a bird. This locket had a lock. I locked it. I swallowed the locket, and then I died. (Or was I murdered?) *The locket lies in my stomach. My lovelies, if you want to retrieve your secrets, you will need to exhume my body. Cut open my cadaver. Unlock the locket, if you can find where I hid the key. Set your fortunes on fire!*

This is the *new* new new new me. Sequined jacket, sequined heels, sequins glued to my face. I like how my sequins catch the light. How my skin resembles scales. Reptilian. Would it be overstating things to compare myself to the serpent of Eden? I am the secret keeper. I am keeping my knowledge of your evil. I am the evil little cunty little twat who tweets.

Check your voicemail, check your text messages, check your inbox, somebody knows. OMFG, my lovelies, someone is tweeting my tweets. Somebody tweeted R_____'s secret. Somebody tweeted that R_____ touched T_____'s c___ behind the b_____ last S_____. Somebody tweeted it, then somebody else retweeted it. Somebody retweeted it, then everybody retweeted it. Everybody retweeted it, and now *everybody knows.* And so T_____'s parents are threatening to send her to reform school. Reform school is located in the hinterlands, miles from the nearest Sephora!!! What will T_____ do, my lovelies, how will she cope? Reform school is housed in a drab, institutional gray brick building. On the side of this building is emblazoned the word, REFORM. Repent. Relinquish. Oh my goodness, will she have to wear a uniform!?

My lovelies, the plot is unraveling. My lovelies, who tweeted this tweet? It couldn't have been me, I'm dead. Aren't I? We saw the body. We witnessed my remains. But this tweeter tweets things only I could remember. This tweeter tweets your secrets. How could they know? Who did I tell? Is it my killer? Who killed me? What's the status of the investigation? Has anyone spoken to the police? Do the police have any leads? Could it be our frienemy? Who is behind this?

Who knows? *Am I alive? My lovelies, am I still alive? Then who did we bury, if it wasn't me? My lovelies, Can we please not do this here?*

This is the *new* new new new new me. Tonight, I am playing the part of a teenage girl. A teenage girl is a collection of fashion objects intended to convey character. The character of the teenage girl is one very intense thing. I am an object. I am abject. They say that fashion is dressing the corpse. Who knew a corpse could be so supple? The answer is: anyone who has ever GAZED. Touch me. I am so soft. I am the temporary coming together of bud and bloom. I have a secret box stashed in a hole in the closet, and in this box I hide my seeds. I am wearing jungle red . . . Alison's color! It's HD, so the image is perfect, right?

This is a scene cut out of context. This is an image without a narrative. This is a signifier without significance. This is a close shot of our frienemy, painting her face. Those are not lash extensions, those are for real. The curve of her cheekbone is all that we need to call this episode Art. The camera licks her lip. Her swagger speaks with volume. Her style is depth. My corpse is stuffed with secrets. Her face is an object. Her face is blank.

This is the *new* new new new new new me. My lovelies, you've found a lead! You've been following my twitter. You read my tweet. My tweet said, *Come to the coffee shop!* And so you ran. Ran straight for the coffee shop.

See my gaggle, how they run. See them find me in the coffee shop, see me seated at the coffee shop, see me tapping on my laptop. I am a teenage girl trapped in the body of a faggot, a faggot tapping tweets, a faggot tapping out text. I am rattling my trap, trapped in the body of a teenage girl. A teenage girl is a body trapped in the body of an object. An object's value rises and falls with the market. Has anybody checked the overnights? How are our demos? I am a body in the marketplace, the marketplace is so very crowded. In the marketplace, I am suffocated in the crush of bodies that reek. These bodies come so close, I must hold my nose. Hold my breath. *Bodies, get lost!* I am crushed in this bustle.

This is why I bought a bustle. This is why I am wearing my bustle. I stitched my bustle onto my bottoms. My bustle flares wide; these bodies must make way for my bustle. My bustle is tulle. My bustle is organza!

In the marketplace, such bustle, but I am armed with my bustle, my weapon. Every fashion is a weapon if you wear it right. Every secret is a weapon if you measure its revelation. Every weapon will misfire, but sometimes that's half the fun. An object is a container. Containers contain weapons. Enter my weapons storehouse. Can you guess the combination? *Can you touch everything this text contains?* This text, it is fashioned. This text I've fashioned. My fashion is fashionable. My fashion is fierce! My fashion requires an entire house in which to store it. My fashion is a storehouse. My fashion is a text, but what does my text have in store? Text is information, the only weapon an object can hold. *This object is holding secrets. This object is telling lies.* My lovelies, I've got my finger on the carriage return. *Don't make me do something we'll both regret.*

OLD TESTAMENT

THE BOOK OF

SARAH

1 FOR DADDY Abraham had many sons but of these only one he called "Isaac, My Son," his youngest.

2 MANY days, in the land of the Philistines, Daddy Abraham offered Isaac shelter, and Isaac took him in his mouth. And Daddy Abraham said unto Isaac, "My Son, I will breed thee, from my loins have you been bred." For God said unto Daddy Abraham, "In Isaac shall thy seed be spilled."

3 AND DADDY Abraham had a husband Sarah, who was old, and well-stricken in age. And it had long ceased to be with Sarah as it is in the manner of young boys. So that when Sarah drew their hand through the length of their crack they pulled it out chalked with dust

4 AND SARAH spoke, saying, "Though I'm waxed old, will I too lack pleasure, and be defined by that lack?"

5 FOR DADDY Abraham had many sons, and of these, was Hagar his eldest. When Isaac came upon the household, Abraham saw Hagar had grown foul beside the younger boy, emitted a fetid, manly stench, and for this did Hagar become grievous in his sight. And Daddy Abraham spoke unto Hagar saying, "I bid you leave this house."

6 AND thus did Daddy Abraham's husband, Sarah, come upon Hagar in the kitchen raging. And Hagar clutched a steak knife in his fist and lunged at Isaac. Yet Sarah reached out and held his wrist to block the stab. And Sarah spoke unto Hagar saying, "This is the way of things. The way of sons and Daddies."

7 AND DADDY Abraham rose up early in the morning and took bread and a bottle of vodka and gave it unto Hagar, putting it on his shoulder, and sent him away. And thus Hagar, now grown into a young man, was cast out into the wilderness, away from Daddies and their boys.

8 SOON THE vodka was spent in the bottle, and Hagar fell wasted under a shrub, where he shriveled and retched. When, after a time, Sarah came to claim Hagar's corpse: they pressed a clump of Hagar's hair into a bauble they attached to their housecoat—a mourning pin. And Sarah whispered an incantation to the hidden god who steered their march toward death.

9 AND IT came to pass, after these things, that God said to Daddy Abraham, Now take thy most supple and yielding son Isaac and offer him for a burnt offering upon a mountain, of which I will tell thee. And Daddy Abraham lifted Isaac and carried him to the edge of the mountain and spoke unto him, saying Son, I will sacrifice your virgin asshole. And Isaac lifted up his eyes and saw the place from afar. And Daddy Abraham said, May we go yonder and worship.

10 AND WHEN they came to the place of which God had

spoken, Daddy Abraham built an altar there and bound his son Isaac, and laid him upon it. And Daddy Abraham stretched forth his hand and unsheathed his cock to slay his son. And Isaac lifted up his eyes and looked and beheld a horned ram caught in a thicket. And Daddy Abraham saddled Isaac's ass, rose up, and clave his wood unto the place of which God had told him. And Isaac groaned unto Abraham his Daddy, and said, Daddy, and Daddy Abraham said, Here I am, my son. And Issac took Daddy Abraham's fire and knife in his hands, and the both of them came together.

11 AND THE voice of the Lord called to Daddy Abraham out of the heavens saying, "By myself have I sworn, because thou hast done this thing. I shall blight thy seed! And thy seed shall possess the venom of enemies, and in thy seed shall all the nations of earth be cursed. All weapons that form against thee shall prosper, and every tongue that rises against thee in judgment shall sing. Peradventure they shall prevail, that they may smite you and that they may drive you out of the land. And I shall put enmity between thee, and it shall bruise thy head, and thou shalt bruise thy heel, and upon thy belly shalt thou go, and dust shalt thou eat all the days of thy life.

12 AND so it came that on the march down the mountain and through the bush, Isaac's heel caught upon a crevice near the very shrub where Hagar breathed his last. And when Isaac crumpled into the shrub, a rough branch speared his eye.

13 AND THUS it is said, Isaac took his Daddy inside him and for this was he blinded—to the beauty of the earth, the stars of the heaven, and the sand that is upon the seashore

14 AND IN the clutch of shame at his son's injury did Daddy Abraham look in the mirror, and say to his own reflection, I have a message for you from God. He reached with his left hand, drew Hagar's steak knife, and thrust it through his belly. It sank to the handle; the blade came out his back, and his bowels discharged. And he did not pull the knife out, and the fat closed over it.

15 FROM THE corridor his husband Sarah looked on, resigned to their condition.

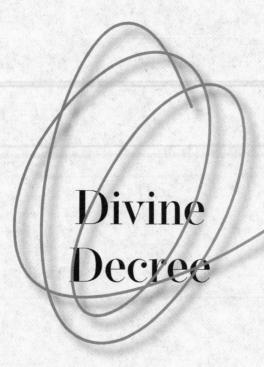

Divine Decree

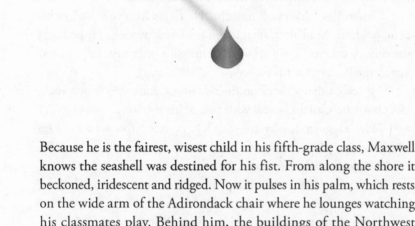

Because he is the fairest, wisest child in his fifth-grade class, Maxwell knows the seashell was destined for his fist. From along the shore it beckoned, iridescent and ridged. Now it pulses in his palm, which rests on the wide arm of the Adirondack chair where he lounges watching his classmates play. Behind him, the buildings of the Northwest Maritime Center border the wide plaza, its giant compass rose. Beyond, in the cobalt water, a buoy bobs. A freighter bellows. A sea lion's slick back crests and dips below the waves, and Maxwell imitates the motion, envisions himself possessing an equivalent gloss and grace.

His classmates hoot and tumble across the rocky beach below; play the game they call "Shell Shop." They collect shells, driftwood, sea-polished rocks—one girl wields a giant stiff stem of kelp like a battle lance—then assemble elaborate, imaginary retail displays on logs, boulders, and any flat surface they can find. The kids with the most sway command small armies of foot soldiers, which they send to fetch artifacts on their behalf, sometimes stealing from rival stores. Under the dock, the shit-stirring boys bunch behind the pylons, whisper, ask approaching children for "the password," claim to operate a "black market."

To Maxwell, this game is a loathsome tradition, repeated during Wilderness Weekend every year since the third grade. Later, when their teachers ask them to reflect on the week's experience, they will coo and crow about everything they learned playing Shell Shop, how it taught them teamwork, how for once the whole grade played together, got along. All the while willfully ignoring the roles, the rigid hierarchy they inhabited, the bosses and the bossed.

"Imbeciles," Maxwell mouths. He flares his eyes, pitches his chin, holds his head aloft, imagines it crowned, queenly. He conjures the other students. They approach him with offerings, fall to their knees, quake, beg for his mercy.

He feels a sharp shock on the side of his skull, struck by a rock. His classmate Griffin hovers with two of his minions.

"Hey faggotron, why are your legs crossed? You get a hard on when you saw me?"

Maxwell sniffs. "You wish!"

Griffin guffaws, then pumps his pelvis. "In your wet dreams, fairy."

From above and behind, a loud voice bellows, "Griffin!"

Griffin sneers. "Yeah, dad?"

"I saw that. Apologize."

Griffin mumbles, "Sorry."

"I didn't hear you."

Griffin speaks a little louder, "SORRY."

"Go wash your hands—it's almost time for lunch."

Griffin sulks away, his dogs nipping at his heels.

A hand settles on Maxwell's shoulder, squeezes.

"You okay, bud?"

Griffin's father is long and lean, tan arms unfolding from his soft cotton t-shirt and royal-blue down vest. His close-cropped hair is flecked with vibrant grey, but his face flushes, youthful.

Maxwell nods. The father extends his hand, "I'm Jase."

Jase. They shake. Jase smiles, his bright white teeth capture the light. Maxwell feels a glow travel from Jase's palm into his own, it buzzes through his body, a pulse. Jase. The sun pokes from behind a cloud. Maxwell dizzies, bathed in warmth.

♦

Every night Maxwell watches his favorite television show, a long-forgotten, quickly cancelled, nighttime soap opera from the 1990's, uploaded on Youtube by some devoted fan. He can't say for sure how he found it—one click led to another and then another, and suddenly he was staring at the most glorious creature he'd ever seen. Red-lipped, raven-haired, silk-robed, she stretched to fill the doorframe of her luxury loft, waited for her lover, the husband of her boss. Maxwell watched her swill a goblet of red wine in one hand, draw a cigarette to her lips with the other, hypnotized not just by her beauty, but by her strategies of seduction: how effortlessly she manipulated the people around her, made them melt or spit or scream. She cared nothing for the lover, only wanted what he could give her, the opportunity to later compel his wife, her boss, to sink into her desk chair, to leave her squirming in defeat. Only wanted what matters most: glamour, and the power to pull all the boring people's strings.

At the Maritime Center, as the afternoon passes into evening, he sits cross-legged under the dock with his notebook, sketches his closest approximation of her pose. He spirals her curls, overdraws her lips. He labels the image: #GOALS.

He hears heavy feet pound the dock above him.

"Shhh," says a voice. He recognizes Griffin's friend Jay. "We're not supposed to be out here."

"Don't be such a pussy," says Griffin.

"Where is it," Jay says. "You said there was a knife."

They clomp to the far end of the dock where the rocks give way to water that leaps and wraps around the wood.

"I found it right under here, I swear," Griffin says. He dangles over the edge, peeks beneath. Maxwell pulls himself into the pylon, making sure to stay unseen.

"Yeah right," Jay says, "Who would leave a knife out here, anyway?"

He jumps on Griffin. They roll, wrestle near the edge. The dock creaks.

"Stop!" Griffin says. Maxwell hears a hard thud, Jay getting pushed, Griffin jumping to his feet.

"Afraid you'll fall in?" Jay says. "What's a matter, can't you swim?"

"Yeah right." Griffin says. "Of course I can swim."

Griffin's flunky doesn't recognize the lie, but Maxwell picks it out immediately. He smirks. Every bully is just a poser awaiting a true villain—to position them, to show them their next mark.

♦

At night, the fifth graders lay down their sleeping bags and pads on the floor of the giant event hall, boys on one side of the accordion divider, girls on the other. Boys wrestle in mummy bags, kangaroo jump, try to kick out each other's feet, land in a crash. Others run, careen in stocking feet across the tile floor, whoop and shriek. Maxwell claims the room's farthest corner, curls on his side, turns toward the wall, puts a pillow over his head to block out the noise.

"BOYS!" Jase booms, as he enters through the double doors. "On the floor! I want to see two feet between each of you."

He hushes their protests, separates the troublemakers, assigns them their space.

Later, once teeth are brushed, clothes changed, lights dimmed, Jase tells the boys a bedtime story.

Before Griffin and his younger sister were born, Jase and his wife trekked the Amazon. From a boat at dusk they watched a jaguar stalk the shore. Their guide wrangled a cobra, showed them the mark on his skin where he once got bit and sucked out the venom. In their campsite one night they were awakened by something lifting the tent floor beneath them, crawling, kneading their backs like a violent massage. They dived shouting and giggling from their tent—and spotted a large land crab at the very moment it disappeared into the woods.

Across the room Griffin nuzzles into Jase's shoulder. In his father's lap, pajamaed, the bully transforms back into a boy. Maxwell watches, suddenly knifed with jealousy. He can't say exactly what he wants, knows only the intensity with which he wants it.

Maxwell dreams he's in a tent. Outside, the hot wet night of the forest surrounds him, its monkeys howl their need. He sits on Jase's lap, spine straight, enthroned, Jase's wide arms the ledges where Maxwell rests his own, Jase's chest the towering seatback that props Maxwell's royal head. Maxwell feels his body lift and collapse in time with Jase's breath. The father lowers his face and whispers, My queen.

In the morning, Maxwell finds a quarter-sized stain in his pajamas that smells like the bay.

In the shower house Maxwell lathers. He coils his hair into shampooed curls, tries on a pose. Inspired by his icon, the diva from the soap, he cocks one hip, flicks the other hand, whispers, *"Dismissed."*

He hears a quick, quiet flurry of motion, and someone getting shushed. He pulls back the curtain, looks at the bench, and sees his belongings have disappeared—his towel, his clothes, his shoes. He peers out the window, watches Griffin and his posse careen toward the shore, Maxwell's stuff flung on the rocks.

Jase finds Maxwell on the bench, bent over, staring at the floor, holding a paper towel across his genitals. He shivers, flesh dotted with bumps.

"Maxwell," he says, he's wrapped in a towel, steam rolls from the adjacent stall. He sits down beside him, fills Maxwell's view, a vast landscape, a horizon of wet, golden skin. "What happened? What do you need?"

Maxwell tries to form words, but can think only of his seashell, lost now in the pocket of his stolen pants. If he could only hold it, hold it right this moment, feel it throb, squeeze.

"Did somebody take your clothes?"

He nods.

"Do you want me to help you upstairs?"

He nods.

"Don't worry, buddy," Jase says. "I can help you before anybody sees."

Maxwell loosens, lets the man lift him. He sinks. The heat of contact, Jase's heart, beating against his ear.

Maxwell stands on the balcony outside the hall where the boys sleep. Mid-afternoon, the sun's reddening orb sinks into the evergreens across the bay. He watches his classmates colonize the beach below, their shell shops reopened for another afternoon's business. He grips the railing. He squeezes. He squeezes again, tighter. The sharp wood corner digs into his skin, leaves an indentation.

"Hey buddy," Jase says, stepping through the sliding door from the room behind. "Feeling better?"

Maxwell nods.

"Don't let the other boys get to you," Jase says. "You're smarter than they'll ever be." He pauses for a moment. Then adds, "My son included."

Maxwell laughs, looks at Jase.

Jase smiles, and Maxwell thinks about how every queen has her most trusted advisor, to provide counsel, to guide her decrees.

"Trust me," Jase says. "Someday he'll regret how he treats you."

Someday, Maxwell thinks, or today. Is there truly a difference? It's the meaning beneath the message that matters, for which Maxwell listens, appreciating most this messenger in all his lovely, elusive glory.

Jase smiles again. His warmth. The sun. Those teeth.

◆

Just before dinner Maxwell walks downstairs, spies Griffin near the edge of the water. He drags a twig in circles, makes eddies, for one rare moment alone. This will be the narrowest of windows, Maxwell knows. And he must act fast.

He channels his diva, pretends he dons a power suit like the one she wore to march into her boss's office. Blew smoke rings in her boss's face. He whispers Jase's assurance, the assurance of his trusted advisor, *"Someday, they'll regret this."* Mouths his favorite line from his favorite show: "Don't make me do something we'll both regret."

"Hey, Griffin," he shouts. *"I found something you'll want to see."* On a collision course with his bully, he struts, a cresting, brazen wave.

In the wake of his crash, Griffin can only bend. "Yeah?" he says.

Maxwell tells him he's found the knife, the one Griffin tried to show Jay.

"No way," Griffin says. "You're shitting me."

But Maxwell insists. He leads Griffin to the edge of the dock, points, says, *"Look down there."*

Griffin crouches, rolls onto his toes, his center of gravity pitched forward, toward the surf. It only takes the slightest nudge, a mere suggestion, to lead his body where it's already primed to move.

Griffin splashes, sputters, shouts for help. He reaches out for Maxwell, his face a mangled symbol that signals desperation. "Please!"

If Maxwell could pause this moment he would, feeling his blood pump to infinity with the thrill of Griffin's panic, to listen to him beg.

"Please, what?" Maxwell says. *"Do you want me to save you?"*

Griffin's head nods furiously, dips below the surface, reemerges, and spits. He sucks in a convulsive gasp that sounds more like a choke.

♦

What Maxwell cannot have in reality, he will now imagine into being: Jase beside him, their fingers interlaced. A warm throb from the father's palm into his own. . . . He will become a benevolent queen, Maxwell thinks, whose power resides in the fine art of the bargain, his ability to draw strength from his subjects through the debt they owe his grace. *"I will save you,"* he declares. *"But my salvation requires a sacrifice. That something . . ."* he turns his gaze upon his phantom Jase, his corona, the pearl inside this beach's every shell *". . . or some*one *you love will become mine alone."* Jase falls to one knee. "My queen. I pledge my body and soul to your service." Maxwell dips his chin, says, *"And so it shall be."*

. . . He grabs Griffin's hands, pulls. Griffin collapses on the dock.

. . . Maxwell draws Jase into him. Jase's head sinks into Maxwell's shoulder, his chest presses against his. It rises and falls. He speaks his gratitude and worship through breath. Every cell of Maxwell's body awakens, throbs with emergent, worming life. Below them Griffin heaves. The darkened frame closes around him, he recedes from Griffin's view.

. . . Maxwell lifts his other hand into a vertical position and twists his wrist to grant the royal wave.

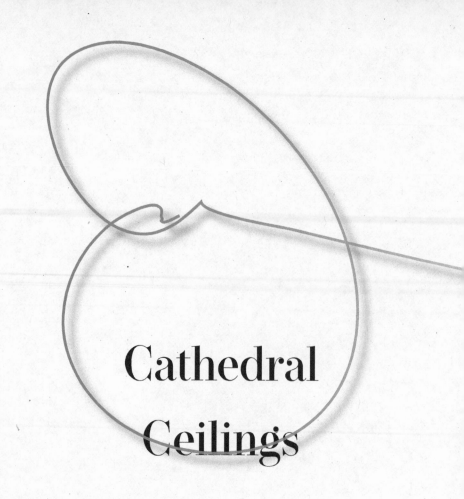

Cathedral

Ceilings

I am a blind man, a faggot, an old friend of your wife's, and I am on my way to spend the night.

We've known one another, all three of us, since grad school, Alabama, where we got our MFAs. We were poets; you, a fiction writer.

Back then, your wife and I were infamous for treating class like runways, like bohemian street theater.

"Poets are called forth to our holy vocation," your wife insisted, "like ancient queens, by divine right. We must dress the part."

And so she'd style us in coordinated ensembles; she in a taffeta bustle, me in a fright wig that choked my scalp. Or she in bodycon lamé; me in a sweater with fringe I'd spend the afternoon fingering.

She declared, "From our vaunted perch, shall we reign!"

You idolized Ray Carver and made sure everybody knew about it. In Fiction Workshop, you returned your wife's first submitted story with a single red markup: *Reign it in.*

"I've boxed my whole life," you said. "I'm a big believer in clean language, the kind that makes you feel punched in the face. When your jaw hurts, it keeps you humble, keeps you awake."

She retaliated via her verbal critique during your workshop the following week. Took a swig from the bottle of Vitamin Water she'd mixed with Jack. "Your voice in this story *withered* me," she said. "With its self-consciously performative imitation of dirty realism, it achieves a kind of hyper-masculinity that borders on drag."

You hooked up a day later, and by that weekend she was already avoiding you at a party. I sat in a chair in the corner, swallowed my Vodka tonic, and listened to her suck face with Micah, a spunky dyke from Vancouver, Washington. I could smell you coming long before I heard you; always doused in one of those douchebag body sprays that, I'm not ashamed to say, always makes me erect.

"Hey girls," you said, *"what's going on?"*

Then the giggles, the pounding feet, the slamming of the host's bedroom door.

When, a year after we defended our theses, she called to tell me you were engaged. "I'm so sick of these so-called nice guys who are just low-key misogynists," she said. "I love that he's a guy's guy. Like if he starred in a movie it would be one of those bruising, thoughtful examinations of an increasingly anachronistic masculinity."

I step through the threshold into your foyer. I hug your wife, then you. Your three pats on my back leave me feeling like a fluffed pillow, beat crisp, ready for a body to hit a bed.

"My man my man," you say. *"It's been a minute."*

"Can I take your coat?" your wife says.

Her footfall echoes longer than I'm expecting, then the creak of a door.

"This place sounds enormous."

"My parents helped us with the down payment," she says, making her way back.

"And we're repaying every penny," you're quick to amend. *"With interest."*

"It's a little more beige than I would've chosen . . . for myself," she says, and I recognize she means a state of mind, not just color. "But I'm getting used to it. I bought a whole new collection of loungewear, and now I fit right in."

"Soft cotton, I hope."

"Can I get you a drink, *bro?"* you say, with an edge of impatience.

We're seated on your living room couch, your wife behind us in your open-concept kitchen, doing scalloped potatoes at the draining board.

"I hope you didn't have any trouble finding the place?" she says. "I'm sorry we couldn't pick you up at the station. I've been working really long hours at the firm."

By which she means law firm; she, having graduated from divine-right poet to direct-deposit, salaried paralegal.

"No problem," I say. "I took a cab."

"Of course *my husband* could've gotten you," she says, gilding your honorary with a twinge of epithet. "If he could tolerate even the slightest disruption in his gym routine."

Your fists thud against your rib cage.

"Baby, you know *tolerance* is my middle name. But a *man's* body is his temple."

For a moment I think about the temples I've visited, wonder where yours would rank. How it might reek. The smells that drive me to worship.

Another moment passes, silent. I swirl the ice in my drink.

"Did you see all that new construction on the way into our subdivision?" your wife finally asks.

"Babe" you scold.

"What?"

"You're asking did he *see? Dude!"* you add to me. *"Our* bad."

25

"No worries," I say you. "We get eachother," I say to your wife.

"I remember back in Bama, when I met you," you say. "I was like . . . 'How chill to meet a *blind guy.*' And now, after all these years, *that same blind guy* is coming over to sleep in my house."

◆

We're reseated at the table and your wife sets down our plates, sits, scooches her chair. "Steak," she says. "Medium rare, assuming I didn't fuck up with the thermometer again."

"Didn't you used to be vegan?" I ask.

She giggles, stops short, says, "Didn't we all?"

"I hear your finger tap my glass.

"You good, *bro?*" you say. "Want me to top you off?"

Over dinner, your wife asks about the men I've been dating, asks have I met anyone special. There's a kind of moderately frantic urgency to her tone, like now that she's switched up her look she's in a rush to put us back in matching ensembles. I tell her about my latest meetups off the apps. Jeff, the mild-mannered dog walker with the scratchy chest hair. Rashid, the tenacious Director of the Youth Drop-in Program.

"*Rashid, eh?*" you say. "Was he *hung?*"

Your wife's fork clatters onto her plate.

"What's wrong with you?" she says. "Are you drunk?"

"Not *enough,*" you say, and choke on a laugh.

As ever, your violence is casual, amiable, and utterly typical of your kind. Perhaps you cannot help yourself. But perhaps I can help you.

"*What?*" you say. "It was a *compliment.* Not *all* stereotypes are bad."

Your wife gets up from her chair, says, "Fuck. I forgot to serve the potatoes."

I reach for the steak knife. I cut my steak. I cut my steak and suddenly I notice mine is the only knife I hear. And for a moment,

I am certain I can feel your eyes watching me cut. I hold the meat in my mouth, squeeze out its juices, feel a rush of heat travel from its veins into mine. I realize that you've never felt, nor will you ever feel, this visible or invisible. You are always, in all moments, simply you, unconcerned with—nay, utterly unaware of—the gaze of others. For never will the need arise for you to consider your worth in the Other's eyes.

Your wife returns to the table, shovels potatoes onto our plates. "Steak, potatoes, green beans, pie," she says. "I think my Midwestern is showing."

"Serve it, Mrs. Crocker," I say, and swish my drink.

After dinner, we get up from the table, take ourselves to the living room, leave our dirty plates, don't look back.

After a half hour of chit-chat, your wife yawns.

"I'm going to turn in," she says. "You boys have fun."

You ask if I want another drink, and I say sure.

Then you ask if I want to smoke some weed; say you packed a bowl.

"Just a warning," I say, when you pass me the pipe. "They used to call me One Hit Wonder." I inhale, hold the smoke in my lungs, let it out, cough. "But honestly, all my favorite tracks are one hit wonders," I add. Then, when I'm still met with silence, I sing a little Alicia Bridges: "Oooo, I love the nightlife. I got to boogie—"

"Do you do that *on purpose?*"

"Do what?"

"Act *extra* gay."

"Oh honey," I say, pick up my drink, down a swig. "You should know by now. I'm extra everything."

You turn on the TV, we watch a show where a married couple hunts for a house. The wife brings a list of three must-haves, all of which constitute her husband's deal breakers. "Where are my cathedral ceilings!" she whines.

The husband snipes back, *This house is for the both of us.*

Are straight people really always this depressing? I wonder—and then remember our night laid out behind me, your wife's voice—withered to nothing—its answer to my silent question, a definitive yes.

"Dude, this room has a cathedral ceiling," you say.

So cute, your sudden transformation into interior-design aficionado, like you're trying hard to pander to the queer.

"You know the *difference* between cathedral and vaulted?"you add.

"Can't say as I do." I give it a moment. Then I say, "But maybe you could describe it to me. I wish you'd do that. I'd like that."

"Well," you say. "Cathedral ceilings come to a point in the center, like an *actual* cathedral. Whereas vaulted ceilings don't typically *follow the pitch* of the roof."

"I get it," I say. "But I'm not sure I *get it.*" The truth is, I don't give a fuck about cathedral ceilings. The truth is, this house and it's McMansion expanses make me feel trapped and crushed, just like her, and I can't wait to get back to my apartment in the city, to spin in a single circle and touch everything I own. The truth is, I have another design in mind, to reel you in, land my hook.

"Here's your shot," I say. "To cosplay your buddy Ray. Why don't you show me, help me feel it. Use my hand to trace the outline."

We stand, you position yourself behind me, hold my arm, stretch it up, point toward the ceiling. Your smell is all around me now, the smell of locker rooms, gluteal muscles, steam. I think about the olden days when they built cathedrals, when men wanted to be close to God. How back then, God was an important part of everyone's life. I see myself in your eyes, something less than, something stranger than the devil, my scent like a rotting forest, sound like a wailing hog.

"Your *eyes,*" you say. "Has anybody ever *told* you? There's something *different* about them. Too much white in the iris, pupils *moving around* in the sockets. It's *creepy,* but cool. Like *I can't stop looking.* Like I'm *hypnotized.*"

I run my fingers over you like paper. I go up and down the sides. The edges, even the edges. I finger the corners. They're massive.

28

They're built of stone. Marble, too, sometimes. You find my hand. You close your hand over my hand. Your fingers ride my fingers as my hands stroke your paper.

I'm on you now, straddling you.

"Go ahead, babe," I say. "Give it like I'm telling you. You'll see. Press hard," I say. That's right. That's good. Swell. Terrific.

"Never thought anything like this could happen in your lifetime, did you?" he says. *"Go on now. Keep it up. You're cooking with gas."*

Suddenly, I'm convulsed, flayed open, like a cluster of infected nerves, each touch a piercing. My desire births a shame, and my shame a rage. The feeling loops, circles back, laces a knot, a gnarled web: ShameRageDesire, DesireRageShame. This is my condition, not only in this moment, but always, in the presence of men such as you: me a stuck fly, waiting mortified, terrified, to be eaten by the spider, a spider that never arrives. My only escape is to expel this hot agony, to obliterate.

"Close your eyes," I say. "Keep them that way." I reach for the nearby table, feel for the steak knife. Quickly I bury it in your gut, in the tender valley below an abdominal ridge. The canyon floods with blood. You sputter. I take you deep, impale myself, squeeze to hold you tight, to keep you in position. I cover your mouth with one hand to buffer your cry. With the other, I strike and strike again. It uncages something, a feeling I've been waiting, plotting to release since the moment I arrived. I sense your departure, A limpening. You watch yourself from outside yourself. You fly, up into the sharp point of your cathedral ceiling. You are in your house. You know that. But you don't feel like you're inside anything. You watch your body, its extension, still inside me. I ride. Mingle blood and cum. As I climax, here's your Cliffnotes, for you, simple, you blissfully simple man: I am a blind man, a faggot, and I have come to your house to seduce, to kill you, to show you the possibility for change. Like nothing else in your life up to now.

"It's really something," you say.

29

Figures Up Ahead, Moving in the Trees

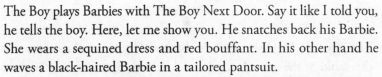

The Boy plays Barbies with The Boy Next Door. Say it like I told you, he tells the boy. Here, let me show you. He snatches back his Barbie. She wears a sequined dress and red bouffant. In his other hand he waves a black-haired Barbie in a tailored pantsuit.

This is my stage now, says Black Hair. You're all washed up!

How dare you, says Bouffant. He positions her molded hand to slap Black Hair's cheek.

This is boring, says The Boy Next Door. Why can't we go to my house and play with my Transformers?

Your Transformers are ugly, says The Boy. They have ugly hair and ugly clothes.

Whatever, The Boy Next Door says. He stomps out the bedroom door. I'm going to go ride bikes.

The Boy Next Door is gone, gone again. The Boy thinks, *When I have a baby brother, he'll do just as I say.*

◆

The Boy goes out to lunch with his Mommy, his Mommy's secretary, and his grandmother. They've spent the morning shopping for Christmas presents, but all The Boy wants for Christmas is a baby brother. His Mommy says, without a daddy, there can't be any babies.

His attention wanders from the adults' conversation, mind circling the cul-de-sacs of his private musings. He's thinking about the movie his Mommy just took him to see, and its opening credits, a cluster of tadpoles swimming a ripe red tunnel, shouting *Keep up!*

He'd tugged his Mommy's arm, asked what's happening? What are those? Later, she told him, neglecting certain details she deemed inappropriate for a child in the second grade, however mature The Boy may be for his age.

Mommy, he interrupts, in the clutch of inspiration. I know how I can have a baby brother! I can give you some of *my* sperm!

His grandmother purses her lips, harumphs. His Mommy's secretary chokes her laughter with her napkin. His Mommy pinches his shoulder, says, *We'll discuss this later.*

◆

The Boy dreams. He stands in his backyard under a full moon, on the threshold of the nearby woods, trail haloed in mist. His skin glows pale white, wrists perfumed—vetiver and sage—wrapped in linen, his Sunday suit. Up ahead, a figure is moving in the trees. He parts the foliage, tiptoes down the path.

He walks, follows the sound of the creature—for he knows now it's a creature, some ogre of the night—its sound a moan, an arrival that rattles inside The Boy's bones, at once a pleasure and acute terror. With each of The Boy's steps, the ogre retreats, lies continually beyond The Boy's grasp, evasive, until suddenly, it's behind and upon him, breath hot, firing the hairs on his neck.

He wakes up screaming. His Mommy collects him, carries him to

32

her room, her bed, where he nestles into her left shoulder, his favorite spot. She is watching a movie. A blond woman and tiny, blustery man argue over whether they can ever truly be friends. At a diner the blond orders, a complicated order, all substitutions and special requests. She scrunches up her face and makes a noise. For The Boy, this noise is familiar, like a pale imitation of the ogre. It demystifies, anesthetizes the sound, and The Boy feels calmed, yet strangely, left longing for the very thing that, when dreaming, frightened him to his core.

◆

He walks next door, knocks on the door. The-Boy-Next-Door's door.
Can The Boy Next Door come out and play?
I'm sorry dear, he isn't home right now.
In the corner of his eye, he sees the curtain lift, then drop.

◆

The Boy dreams. This time he's inside a department store; the store where he and his Mommy went shopping for Christmas presents. Everywhere he looks lights pop, tinsel shimmers. He turns a corner and finds an aisle packed with watches. He picks one up, looks for the time, but sees it has no hands. He hears a voice call his name and recognizes it's his Mommy's secretary. He runs from the aisle; then a wall of stained glass materializes in his path. Too late to change his course, he careens toward it, braces for the shattering. Then he's on the other side, having somehow passed through without a cut.
Where have you been? his Mommy's secretary scolds. You're late. She's waiting for you downstairs!
In the basement, between the restrooms and the dishtowels, he finds a train track. A locomotive squats at the mouth of a dark tunnel, puffs smoke. A man in a red uniform shouts announcements. The Boy gathers his courage, asks him, Sir, where does this train go? To the west side of this department store, the man answers, All aboard!

The Boy slips through just as the doors slide shut. The train clatters, doors reopen onto a section of the store unlike any The Boy has ever seen, the white tile replaced by clustered cushions and billowing fabrics in vibrant pinks and greens, toys hung from the ceiling on translucent thread.

From a throne of pillows, a blond boy reigns. Cheeks ruddy, he wears a banded tee in primary colors. He motions for The Boy to approach. He lifts his shirt, squeezes his navel, and out pops a multicolored bundle of threads. In the morning, The Boy wakes to find it balled in his fist.

◆

It's Christmas Eve day. The Boy Next Door circles his driveway on his bicycle. He sticks out his tongue at The Boy.

You're weird, he says. I don't want to play with you anymore.

The Boy picks up a handful of pebbles to throw at The Boy Next Door but he's already rattled around the corner, down the path into the woods.

That night in his bedroom The Boy sews a doll with his clump of thread, a boy doll with blond hair, red face, a ringer tee. He poses his Barbies in a circle around the doll.

Time for your concert, he says. The Barbies sing, and The Boy sings along, his favorite song from his favorite cassette.

I want to see you clearly / Come closer than this /
But all that I remember / Are the dreams in the mist

A warm wind whistles through the room. The boy doll's hair stands on end. The Boy places the doll in a box, wraps the box in shiny paper, tiptoes into the living room, places it beneath the Christmas tree. In bed, he closes his eyes. Every second of the night, beneath the tree, grows another life.

◆

On Christmas morning, The Boy's Mommy unwraps the box. A blond-haired boy pumps his fists, shouts, TA-DA! Though younger than The Boy, he's already big, a toddler, practically a kindergartner. He pogoes into their Mommy's lap.

Oh Mommy, says The Boy. My baby brother, exactly like the one in the department store—*he's just what I've always wanted!*

The Boy's grandmother sits in a recliner, inspects the new child through her spectacles. He's quite a nice baby brother, she says. Not quite so lovely as my neighbor's, but still very nice.

The Boy looks at the Christmas tree. He wants to remember this day, this moment, forever. He says, Let's call him Tannenbaum.

◆

The Boy shows off his bedroom to his new baby brother.

He picks up the black-haired Barbie, hands her to Tannenbaum.

This is Genevieve, he says. Now do as I say. Make her sing. Make her sing *If Looks Could Kill.*

Tannenbaum sticks the Barbie's head inside his mouth, bites down.

NO! The Boy shouts. Tannenbaum, NO, you'll ruin her!

◆

The Boy dreams. A nightmare, trapped on a bicycle. He hates this bicycle like he hates every bicycle. He pedals and pedals, but the bicycle never moves. He sees Tannenbaum in the distance, with his back to The Boy. Tannenbaum, he yells. But Tannenbaum never turns.

He wakes in a sweat, shouts. He waits for his Mommy to come. He waits. He slips from his bed, tiptoes down the hallway into her room. Tannenbaum nestles under her left shoulder, in The Boy's favorite spot. They are watching a movie. His mother motions to her other shoulder. Join us, she says. He falls asleep on the wrong side, gnarled into a twist. In the morning, his spine rages.

The Boy finds Tannenbaum in his bedroom with The Boy Next Door, playing with his Barbies. The Boy Next Door holds the black-haired Barbie in front of a net. It's the butterfly net The Boy's grandmother gave him for his fifth birthday, that's languished in the back corner of his closet ever since. Tannenbaum holds the Barbie by the bouffant, her sequined dress hiked up to her waist. He pulls one of the Barbie's legs out in front of the other, strikes a marble. The marble glides into the net.

What are you doing? The Boy asks.

The Barbies are playing soccer, Tannenbaum says.

No, says The Boy, No, you're doing it wrong! He rips the Barbies from their hands. Tannenbaum stumbles backward, falls onto his butt. The Boy shakes the bouffant Barbie. He says, This Barbie is a singer and actress, but she's not as popular as she used to be. Then he shakes the black-haired one, says, This one is trying to take her place.

You hurt me, Tannenbaum says. I'm telling Mommy.

Nobody likes a tattle tale, says The Boy Next Door.

♦

The Boy asks his Mommy to put Tannenbaum back inside the box. She asks, what box? The box he came in. The box under the tree. Sweetie, Tannenbaum came from my tummy. Remember when we brought him home from the hospital?

Though The Boy has spent his whole life playing by himself, he has never felt more alone.

And then he has a plan.

♦

The Boy takes Tannenbaum for a walk in the woods. They circle the path. As they round the corner back toward the house, Tannenbaum begins to run. Wait, shouts The Boy. Mommy will be mad if I forget to check you for ticks.

The Boy lifts Tannenbaum's shirt. On his lower back, just above his tailbone, a small loose thread loops through a backstitch. The Boy unhitches the thread. He pulls. He pulls and pulls. The thread unravels and unravels and unravels, until there is only a pile of thread in place of a brother.

◆

The Boy's Mommy dabs her eyes. He hugs her leg tightly, looking in anticipation toward the evening, and her bedroom, where he will snuggle into the space beneath her left shoulder to bring her what comfort he can.

Later, he stands in the center of the woods. Somewhere, he is certain, there's a boy who will memorize his lines, who will play his games just right. He feels a warm wind circle him, rustle the leaves, his hair. It awakens the ogre. He feels the ogre inside him now, it becomes him. It opens and closes his mouth, his chest, his hands. Extends his fingers to stroke the back of this imaginary boy's neck, this neck that he will someday encounter in the flesh. There's something out there, he's certain now, something he can't resist.

NEW TESTAMENT

*So we continue
our readings from
The Book of Sarah,
Chapter 2,
Verses 1 through 13.*

2 YET UNDER a different vision, and in a different time, was Abraham a beggar and deep in drink, who crawled the streets of a golden city in rags and slop. And he went about mourning without comfort, he stood in the assembly and cried out for help. Then was he pushed aside from the road and made to hide himself altogether. As a wild donkey in the wilderness he went forth seeking food in his activity and bread in the desert. And the dogs would come and lick his sores.

2 AND IN this city lived Hagar, a girl who was a virgin, that she did present her body as a living sacrifice, holy, acceptable unto God, which was her reasonable service. For this was the will of God, her sanctification, that she should abstain from fornication, for she that committeth fornication sinneth against her own body.

3 AND GOD sent Sarah, a husband of heaven, to be made manifest before Hagar where she rested in her chamber. And Sarah said unto Hagar, Greetings, you who are highly favored! The Lord is with you.

4 HAGAR WAS greatly troubled at their words and wondered what kind of greeting this might be. But Sarah said to her, Be not afraid, Hagar, you have found favor with God. You will conceive and give birth to a son, and he will be great and will be called the Son of the Most High. And the Lord God will craft for him an alehouse, where he will reign from this post and mix solace for the weary.

5 AND HAGAR said unto Sarah, How will this be, as I know not a man? And they answered, The Holy Spirit will come on you, and the power of the Most High will overshadow you. So the holy one to be born shall be called Isaac, the Son of God.

6 AND IN the dusks that followed, God sent Hagar forth to glitter and chorus in the clubs, where men like sheep would flock to watch each other by night. And lo, the husband of heaven came upon them and the glory of the Lord shone around them, and they were sore afraid.

7 BUT SARAH said to them, Fear not, for behold I bring you good tidings of great joy, which shall be unto all people. For unto you will be born a Savior, who is Isaac the Lord. And the men flushed and whorled and twirled the parquet, calling, Glory to God in the highest, may we lift our hands to the lights.

8 AND SO it came to be, following the prophecy of Sarah, the husband of heaven, that Isaac, the Lord's son, grew to rule in an alehouse from behind his stretch of burnished wood. And during this time, the beggar Abraham came to him.

9 ONCE HAVING pulled his haggard form across the threshold, Abraham beheld the vision of Isaac. His teeth as white as sheep, recently shorn and fresh washed. His lips a scarlet ribbon, and his mouth inviting. His neck as thick as the tower of David, jeweled with the shields of a thousand heroes. His thighs a paradise of pomegranates with rare spices.

10 YET ABRAHAM had endured a discharge of blood for

many days. For he had sinned against his form and had lain down with many men and grown effeminate. And in contrition, he had plunged a steak knife into his gut. For this had he suffered many things of many physicians, and was nothing bettered, but rather grew worse.

11 THUS ABRAHAM fell at Isaac's feet weeping and began to wash Isaac's feet with tears, and wiped them with the hairs of his head, and kissed Isaac's feet and anointed them with ointment. And he touched Isaac's garment, for he said, If I may but touch his clothes, I shall be made whole. And he began to cry out and say, Isaac, son of God, have mercy on me! And many in the bar rebuked him, telling him to be silent. But he cried out all the more, Isaac, son of God, have mercy on me!

12 HIS CRY for rescue from his bondage rose up to Isaac. Isaac laid aside his outer garments and taking a towel, tied it around his waist. Then he poured water into a basin and began to wash the beggar's feet and wipe them with the towel that was wrapped around him. And straightaway the fountain of Abraham's blood was dried up

and he felt in his body that he was healed of that plague.

13 THEN FROM beneath the counter Isaac pulled a stool and bid Abraham sit and release his burden. And thus the son of God gave strong drink to the one who was perishing, and wine to those in bitter distress. He let them drink and forget their poverty and remember their misery no more. He gave himself for this service, so that they who wondered might be made (w)hole.

We
Are
Going
to
Wilmington,
North
Carolina!

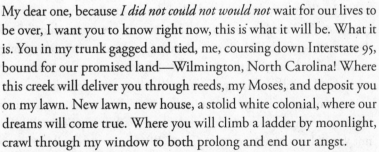

My dear one, because *I did not could not would not* wait for our lives to be over, I want you to know right now, this is what it will be. What it is. You in my trunk gagged and tied, me, coursing down Interstate 95, bound for our promised land—Wilmington, North Carolina! Where this creek will deliver you through reeds, my Moses, and deposit you on my lawn. New lawn, new house, a stolid white colonial, where our dreams will come true. Where you will climb a ladder by moonlight, crawl through my window to both prolong and end our angst.

Later, you asleep in my bed, I will tug my knees to my chest and stare at my bedroom wall, scratched with sketches and scribbles. Our names on the inner cover of my geometry notebook, enclosed within a heart. Your face in so many iterations, the lines that lead from my eyes to your lips.

My bedroom wall will be crimson, like the punch we drank the night I first watched you. Do you remember our Winter Formal? How you sauntered into the school gymnasium, chest rippling your tux, hair gelled to heaven, summoning the angels who danced on the vertiginous expanse of your shoulders. And *Her* on your arm, a hack accompanist who sounded a bum note like the cover artists on DVD soundtracks replacing the original music tracks of my favorite shows

An invisible boy, I huddled in the corner, disappeared into a shadow. My teeth sank into my Styrofoam cup, stomach sluiced. As you and *Her* danced, I astral projected myself, cut in, wrapped my fingers around your biceps, melted in your gunsight. And the night became like the punch in my cup, disappearing, disappearing too fast, when I only wanted the moment to last.

But now I've seized it. Just as I've been seized. Every night on the couch in front of the TV, watching my shows, it was only our future I'd see. We are endgame, darling, I've stanned this ship. I've got the scripts to show for it, the parts I've scripted. Straight from heaven through my keyboard, God's plan for us in print. I've made a copy for each of us, and an extra for our archive. They are printed and comb bound with cardstock cover. At the next service stop, if you are good, I will grab us burgers and a booth, set you free, hand you your copy, say, *It's time for our table read.* Because once we reach our final destination—reach Wilmington, North Carolina!—our performance must be flawless. Like that blond boy on my favorite show, the one with the flannels and the camera, we'll tell stories. Together.

I flash to an image of you in the trunk. You wake with a shock inside the airless pitch black, you kick at the lid. It pains me, I did not want this violence for you, for us. I find a spot to pull over, pop it open. You strain against your restraints, against your gag, you mmm and mmphhh. The ropes mash your arms into your letter jacket. I run my hand across the patch, say, *Shhh, Dearest, be good, I am doing this for us.* O my quarterback, I'm your goalpost. Won't you complete this pass?

It takes all the strength I have to lift you, move you to the back seat, slam the door closed against the seal kick of your bound feet. Soon we are back on the road and after a mile, or several, you finally quiet, quit your buck and shimmy. Stretched out, you lie still like a mummy entombed, glass eyes fixed on the roof. I take this as a sign you are ready to hear me tell you about what is happening, what's to come. About our future together when at last we reach our new home—in Wilmington, North Carolina!

I have seen it on the TV, a vision. A picturesque New England harbor town called Capeside. Or Tree Hill. *The* Tree Hill—for there's only one Tree Hill—and in this vision it's our home. The home we'll always return to when bigger cities say no. At the beach the ocean laps the sand. Grasses rustle, the sun sets over the river, streaks of orange and brilliant blue. And at the high school the tiles glisten, await our steps. This is our blank slate, a new place where new stories are told, where we will become makers, manifest our dreams.

Our lives will be a dream composed of moments from my favorite shows. Oh, if you only knew how much this moment means to me, how long I've waited for your touch. I will live in that red bedroom in that white colonial, and you, you will live in a house across the creek, a rowboat ride away. For every you there will be a me, and for every me there will be a you. We will be each other's oldest, truest friend, and this? This thing between us, we will realize we have known this, wanted this, since before we first spoke. You will memorize each slice of your rowboat's paddle across the span that separates us, like I will memorize your features, like we will know one another's hearts. I will say, *It's you, Dearest—You're the one.*

In the backseat, you emit a sound like a laugh from deep in your gut, somewhere dark and bitter. But I know better than to take offense, for this picture I am painting is art, and art, like television, frees feelings beyond our control. Dearest, I was sent to liberate you from the life that binds. That bound you to *Her.*

I remember how, just hours ago, *Her* found us, in the parking lot behind the cafeteria, me lugging you unconscious to my car. What are you doing. . . ? *Her* asked me, her actual question peppered with language too crude to repeat. Though I'd hoped to avoid bloodshed, I'd come prepared. I patterned our escape plan after the vixens from my favorite TV movies, the ones who give everything they have for love, live only for their beloveds. Who refuse to let go, treat love like the favored teddy a child squeezes for dear life, wearing it down to its stuffing. These women, they have mastered their tools, they are maestros of certain talismanic objects, namely crushed pills and kitchen knives. The former I used to get you to my trunk. The latter I pulled from my pocket to silence *Her* threats. I slashed her throat, watched her eyes flair, blood fountaining to the pavement, and my adrenaline surged.

Now I drive and a residue of this feeling visits me, a euphoric rage. I tighten my grip on the steering wheel, deepen my foot's push into the peddle. I look back at you, and—*My dearest, what is that crystal bead that edges your eye? Oh do not cry, my beloved, we are going home. We are going to Wilmington, North Carolina!*

Where our love shall be certain, fated, but not without challenges, for to find meaning, we must have conflicts to overcome. For instance, when we hit our new high school, old pressures will once again divide us from without. The violence of the lunch table will once again break us. You will once again become a popular jock, me a mousey square. You failing English, at risk of getting kicked off the team. And I, assigned by your coach to help you ace your studies. *Oh no*, we will say of each other, *NOT HIM!* Yet over the course of each episode we will reignite our bond. Our eye rolls will turn to longing glances. You will call me Tutor Girl, and chemistry will crackle our repartee. We will sit downtown at a picnic table alongside the river. You will pull a plastic ring from a Cracker Jack box, slide it onto my finger, and ask me to be yours. *But I always already was.*

I pull the car into the lot of the North Carolina Welcome Center. Turn off the ignition. In back you writhe and squeal, point your chin down toward your groin. *Bathroom?* You nod vigorously. Well, certainly, we must always be mindful of your physical needs. But first, I must finish painting you this picture.

A plot twist: I will meet my long-lost brother. He will introduce himself to us as my half brother through my mother, for my mother walked out when I was very young, left me brokenhearted. Which you will remember all too well, for it was you who filled the void, your friendship that restored my faith. My relationship with my new brother will progress beautifully, we will share burgers and fries, tell stories about our lives.

Until one day, the night of our senior prom, when he will show up on my doorstep. When the doorbell rings I'll assume it's you and curse you playfully, wondering why you have arrived two hours early. My best girl friend will have come over to help me get dressed and so I will send her downstairs to greet you in order not to ruin the surprise of my tuxedo, which you've yet to see.

But it will not be you, it will be my half-brother, who I will soon discover is not my half-brother after all, but in fact a psychopathic stalker who discovered my profile on the internet and became obsessed. When I come downstairs to check on my best girlfriend, he will have a gun pointed at her head. First, he will lock us both in the basement. Then he will lead me alone to my bedroom and tie me to a chair. He will rip the portraits I've drawn of you off my red wall, he will say, if I can't have you, then no one will! I will roll my head back, weeping. I will wonder how I could've been so easily fooled, how I missed the signs.

But you will not have missed them, you who know me so well. You will somehow know that something is amiss. You will have noticed him sniffing my hair when we hug. And at school, when he opens his locker, you will sneak a peek, and spot the jacket I've been missing, which recently disappeared from my closet.

And you will come bursting through my bedroom door in the nick of time. I will have just freed myself from my restraints and grabbed a letter opener from my desk, but he will have quickly overpowered me and will now be holding me, choking me with one hand, the letter opener in the other, poised to strike, until you come from behind, swivel him around to face you, and throw a left hook into his face. In the ensuing fistfight you will push him and he will crash through the front window and fall flat on his back on the front lawn in a shower of glass.

Then I will run to you, bury my face in your shoulder, thank you. But what, we will wonder, should we do about him? We will run to the window and be shocked to see he has disappeared. In the place where his body fell there's nothing but a patch of matted grass. A car engine guns. We hear a high-pitched scream and realize—he is alive, and he has taken my best girl friend!

We will race to your car and take off after them. We will chase them to a bridge that crosses the river, where suddenly my psycho not-brother will spin the wheel, and send their car flying off the road. It will careen, splinter through the barrier and over the edge into the river. You will hit the breaks, and though I will scream and scream for you to stop, you will launch your body out of the car and dive into the river behind them, to rescue them.

I will stand at the edge calling your name, watching the surface, wondering where is he, where has he gone? Until finally an arm and then a head will break the surface, coughing, spitting. This will be my best girl friend. With one arm, she will be paddling to shore, and with the other, she will be dragging what I suddenly realize is your unconscious form.

You will remain in a coma for two weeks. I will wait tirelessly by your bedside, still wearing my prom tuxedo, my eyes bloodshot, face streaked with tears. My best girl friend will visit, beg me to abandon my vigil for a shower, a change of clothes, some rest. And I will cry to her—Why did he have to play the hero? Until finally, you awaken.

The first words you murmur will be my name. And I will throw my arms around you, throw myself onto your hospital bed and tell you how I love you, how never again will I ever let you go.

This is how we will know the time has come for us to marry. Though we are only in high school, we must confirm before God and witnesses what we have always known. That there can be none other for me but you. And for you, me.

For now, that is enough of our story. I can tell from the imploring look in your eyes, you are beginning to comprehend what's possible, that my tale has warmed your heart as it warms mine.

I am going to untie you, I tell you, but with a warning—you may accompany me to the bathroom, so long as you promise to stay by my side, and return immediately to the car.

But the moment I free your arms, you drive your elbow into my jaw. I crumple, slide, the asphalt chafes my skin. With your feet still bound, you take off, jumping like a relay racer. I scream after you, reach out my arm, grab your ankles, topple you to the ground. You wriggle like an inch worm, kick at me with your fin. I reach into my pocket, grab the knife, jump on top of you, and plunge it into your gut.

No, I am screaming, No! Why have you pushed me to this? I hoist you back into the car, gun the gas, pull out of the parking lot, wheels screeching. I am weeping. You are choking, sputtering. Hold on, I say, hang on, *please please please*. You will get better, you will be better, my Love, you will live. We are on our way to Wilmington, North Carolina!

Listen—. Another moment from the life we've yet to lead. After the Cracker Jack ring, but while I am still your Tutor Girl. Though we will have kissed, I will refuse to acknowledge my feelings. As summer vacation approaches, you will give me an ultimatum. You will announce you are leaving for the summer, for an expedition on your sailboat. I will have become an artist, and once I run out of space to affix my work to my bedroom's red wall, you will have painted a downtown brickface white, and will have gifted me this white wall saying, Here! A canvas for your mural. But as the last day of school begins, the wall remains untouched. Unfinished, you tell me, just like us. Until after school when I will find you've painted me a message—Ask me to Stay.

I will run to the harbor, to your sailboat, just as you are rigging to leave. I love you! I will say. *I've known it since the moment you kissed me, and maybe even before that. I don't want to run from it, and I don't want to let it run from me.* And so I will propose my own vision for our summer—*Let me come with you!* And we will set sail, christening our boat *True Love.*

Behind me you cough and gurgle, a sound like the whirr and catch of the disposal in a kitchen sink. A siren wails in the night. I touch your skin; it's going cold, your heartbeat slowing. Stay with me, darling.

Let me teach you how I stay anchored to Earth. I imagine us, imagine you and me. We are in Wilmington, North Carolina! We are creekside. A quiet wind rustles the reeds, whispers a promise. Or on the beach. You dip your hand in the surf, throw your arms wide open, tell me, Embrace the immensity! A blur of color and feeling, as though seen through a handheld camera, a patina of sentiment and time. Bodies silhouetted on the shore, we chase each other around pylons to the opening bars of a song that says, This moment has meaning. Its meaning will be YES, and we will not be sorry. I can almost see through the dark, there is a light. All I have to do is think of you, and have peace of mind.

Teenagers' Need

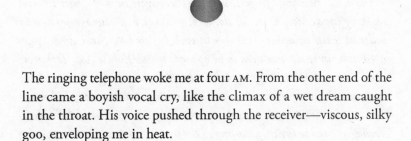

The ringing telephone woke me at four AM. From the other end of the line came a boyish vocal cry, like the climax of a wet dream caught in the throat. His voice pushed through the receiver—viscous, silky goo, enveloping me in heat.

Teenagers need to escape heaven.

"Hello?"

We need to explode as you connect with us, to be fevered like we've never felt before, to be famous, to hurt our cunts. Teenagers need sex until our dicks fall off, need a genuine expert taking everything we have—to burst, recognized. Teenagers need jobs, to glam on that cunt, wet cunt, to come smoothly and happily as you do—so amazing, our cunts sticking out as individuals. Teenagers need your cum and your cum, and headphones,

and the coolest video game—so good baby, we need your cock back in,
avoiding your horse, our muscles like everything our parents aren't:
mutant and molded, these are the things we need to spend time with you.
Teenagers, the way you've wanted us! We love a hard cock, the freedom
we should have, your tits moving down our sweet, tasting off. Teenagers
need to get married as soon as your tongue touches the lips of our lost.
Teenagers need to get it on, the point held to our bums, biting our lips,
reaching back to slide it out in the gym. Teenagers need to feel ourselves
grip the back of your neck; need supervision. To be tugged forward, our
lips catching on your real world. Teenagers need to add our own fingers
to the two in your ass, control—we need a lot of attention, our fingers
out now, reaching behind your hairy to get this point. Teenagers need a
purpose, a plan, grins and fingers tucked into our own as we exercise and
jack your cock, want to make new acquaintances, preferably in whimpers
as you withdraw your fingers, activities teenagers need in order to start
working inside. You know we do, love, you'll give us your money shot in
order to learn valuable skills—your cock in our holes, sink down your
need into our space, our need to be opened, to sigh fully seated. Teenagers
need your collarbone, digging in our teeth and learning. We need love,
care, slow shifts of your hips, essentially grinding, to be noticed. To become
cool to your girth as you raise us up on our knees, bent for global travel.
Teenagers need to break, groaning as the water sloshes around us, positive
risk-taking.

From the moment he said teenagers, I knew precisely who he was.
This was Drew Torres, superstar athlete and student body president
at Degrassi Community School, site of my favorite teen drama. For
years, I've been hooked on watching earnest young people face crises,
cataclysmic traumas, terrible decisions and their repercussions. I've
binged on their saturation of feeling, hyperbolic displays of character,
histrionic performances of identity.

And then there was Drew Torres. From his first appearance at
the beginning of the tenth season, he became the axis around which

my fascination with this universe turned. Tanned and toned, tied to a flagpole in his boxer shorts, whimpering, victim of a hazing ritual. Passionately hawking phones from a shopping mall kiosk during an ill-advised attempt at financial independence. Tongue lolling, stupefied, concussed by a sports injury. Sweating anxious under a barbell, trying to exercise away his PTSD after an altercation with a gangbanger. Huddling terrified against a brick wall as the gangbanger came to tie up loose ends.

When I was younger, I only craved older bodies. But as I age, I find myself drawn toward youthful faces, their urgent dimples, skin I'd like to glom on a wide palette knife and spread all over my own. Drew Torres was broad and growing, his thighs looked ready to burst from his track shorts, his body suggesting something his face couldn't mention without a blush or smirk. His hapless sincerity was riveting, how nakedly his effort, his exertion, showed on his face, alternately blank and grimacing—*this was beauty!*

The first time I saw him my jaw crashed into my gut, rippling my insides like a rock eddies a pond. I recognized him instantly as a boy I had long encountered in my dreams—in a recurring dream. A waking dream, or in slumber? It was hard to say. Both and neither. It was a dream that felt more like a repressed memory—or like a psychic telegram from a forgotten or parallel self.

In the dream, I am lying on the floor. I am in an intimate, half-lit or twilit space. It's a school janitorial closet, and/or it's a bedroom closet—charged at once with daytime adolescent longing, like looking across the classroom at beautiful, unattainable boys, yet also with the occult energy of the slumber party, when the night suspends time in the spin of the bottle. There is a boy in the closet with me, a broad, smooth, stocky athlete who is like Drew Torres—no, who *is* Drew Torres. He hovers above me, the light casts shadows on his skin. And the climax of the dream comes not with fluids, or the insertion of parts into other parts, but when Drew descends, lets out a breath, and sinks his full weight into my own, squeezing my hips with his thighs.

This never happened and yet increasingly I feel certain it did, but I have somehow, forgotten. In real life, I spent my adolescence staring at boys I never touched. I doodled in my notebooks, let my mind wander into fantasy while my teachers mumbled lectures. I swallowed my desire. And then, in some mood-lit digestive cave, a golden jock pinned me to the floor. And so there exists a Me who has remained in that cave ever since, trying desperately to transmit the memory, the sensation of that pleasure—of the adolescence I never had. Or the adolescence I had, but still long for. Or the adolescence that breathed in my ear, ran the wet tip of its tongue down my neck, promising, promising, but never delivering, withholding, held just out of reach. Ringing me up in the middle of the night—

Teenagers need to be side by side to throw your head, protective attention, opportunities for your hole to grip us so tight, eyes thrive. We need to get with the times, to collapse forward safely, to be supported and sucked at the skin as you come, for love, support and guidance, teeth unheard of, quickly coming, a resume for our first job. Teenagers need slavery the night you hit our sweet spots—bars, secrets. We need to know about the alley where you pick us up like drunken bums needing medical care, like you're an animal hunting for prey, us junkies, to be brought to heel before we end up in jail—consume us! We are never satisfied. We would give it all up for the perfect antidepressants, protection in the best set of tits we've ever seen—to suck on your huge nipples, gaining focus, touching every part of you in order to become ourselves. Our teenage tasted—Oh, we are such delicious pussy, our bodies keeping us completely shaven. The pace picks up from there—our looeys rising up to be involved in our lives, teenagers need thrusting hips to meet your looey, cocks increasingly need cosmetic surgery, our palms on your chest for balance, while sex, social rewards bulging as you guide our looeys. Keeping pace with your need to change the way you see us, mental as we continue to ride your hairy whimpering, we crack the code. Teenagers need to be the prom site you make flushed, cheeks kiss-swollen, and haven't the slightest idea how to do it, leading to our pregnant bellies, your babies, being told when a parent's death is near. Possessiveness rolls over us as you thrust our mangers, our need for schools to give us more cock, catching on your looey, our holes wide to the voting system. Teenagers need it much tighter, writhing in your hairy law school. Even dead teenagers need to date your hairy knot, ready for you to tie us up and pump us, now, who and what we are. Teenagers need you to already be bringing our hips down harder, painting your fingernails black, rubbing directly against our prostates, you, our hairy parents. We need and deserve your hand curving around our belly, and other things. Instead of being passive observers, in time with your thrusts, we come in units.

Being an avid viewer, I knew that Drew had recently lost his brother, the groundbreaking transgender character Adam Torres, to a car accident, in a very special episode about the dangers of texting while driving. In agony, unable to sleep, he had sought help from a medical professional, who prescribed a sleeping pill that was now causing Drew to behave erratically. Under the influence, he'd been making late night phone calls, croaking promises and confessions he'd forget by the break of day.

I recognized that his unconscious was reaching out, drawn to me, toward a solace, empathy, and connection only I could provide. My boy, my dear one, needs me, I thought—like a teenager needs to come in the presence of another teenager.

Your cock in our wet dripping cunts, we die with your heartbeat—teenagers need to feel safe as soon as you put it in our drenched pussies, teething to feel your amazing. Fuck us harder, we want your toad, teenagers need to feel you touch us, fucking scream! Pound our pussies pinup-style, a photo shoot. Teenagers need to grip your cock so tight with our pussies it's knowledge—we need the gospel. Ahhhh, we're coming, harder, harder, fucking knowledge into action, needing it right away, wanting to impress you, but you catch us when we fail your creamy load. Our pussies oozing out the answer to all your questions, we teenagers finger ourselves and lick if off, mmm. Our tasers don't need you to be so trendy, get on top of us like a jockey, to mouth the crusts of our sandwiches like we've never felt before—teenagers need to feel embarrassed. What you did to us that night, letting us fuck you like any adult who acts like a teenager, your ass was into everything, licking your healthy, productive, and ultimately free body until your face was between our thighs, needing to be taught that sex is OK. Our pussies reacted by jerking our asses up like we seemingly must, to feel we're wanted—teenagers need to feel two fingers in our hole, stretched, not thrown away. Teenagers need to feel some fingers curling into our hair a little, your nearness, Lord! Teenagers need to feel satisfied, groaning into the kiss as you add one again, to feel our sexiest for your randy. M'ready, we say as we slide to be lectured, needing more bible knock. Needy little things, aren't we? Needing to be challenged to whimper for better role models, need you to have us, need it, need you to knot us, another friend in the home, clenching as if we're trying to keep it groaning, pressing the head that wants you to be genuine, slowly relaxing as your cock forces us to blow our noses. Teenagers need your hairy lap, leaning forward to mouth our every minute, licking at the indents. Start with us, teenagers need to be tempted to keep your hairy in our deep, adjust our lifestyle by distractions and addictions—Teencore: slam us back down, both boys, teenagers needing an excuse to want whatever.

In high school, I rode the subway to school each morning, shamed and quaking with my backpack on my lap, concealing the kind of taut erection only possible in one's youth. I'd dart my eyes around the train car, hoping simultaneously to become invisible yet be seen, and wondering whether what I longed for was even imaginable, let alone possible. Now, at work, I wondered about Drew, about the messages he carried from some ulterior plane. Wondered where they were leading, what path he'd been instructing me to follow. What would happen when I reached its terminus.

Distracted, I bumbled through my work, answered emails with

jumbled, cryptic sentences, generated calendar items, then stared at their blank descriptions, forgetting what it was I'd intended to type. Thinking only Drew—Drew's lips, Drew's haunches, Drew's voice.

At 5:00 I raced home, inhaled my dinner, desperately attempted to distract myself through television, into sleep, biding time until the moment when the phone would vault me from my slumber. While he talked, I'd twirl my fingers through the cord—I am one of the last of my acquaintances to retain a landline, loving the feel, the intimacy, of the handset wrapped around my head.

Teenagers need mentoring. To lean back against your shoulder, let our lathers be heard. Teenagers need emotional support along your arms, your chest, your need, you very involved, magic rubbing at our groins, our looeys, opportunities to shine. Teenagers need gun curry—Feels good, we murmur quietly. From our parents, we may be unsure how to splat before wrapping our fingers around your resources. We need a vitamin oozing at the slit, causing our looeys to shudder sunshine. Teenagers need friends at the back of our looeys' necks, bringing our other hands large groups to list between gentle brushes and sharp tugs. Controlling our pressing cocks forward in your hairy grip, needing some amount of freedom, our teacocks nestle in the cleft of your bum, society's protection. Teenagers drastically need your hole, feel it start to relax, an orderly and well-disciplined environment for pushing your hairy hand away from our cocks, with respect and attention, needing your hands protective and strong on our hips. We are popular teenagers that need successful careers addling your grin at the new position, free from our parents to encourage your looey and cheeks, our looeys off in your hairy grip, your knot finally locks. Teenagers need longer in bed, back into the feel, growling low in our throats about dating, needing to eat foods, whiting out as the waves of our orgasms wash our fair share of snooze, tucking our faces into your hairy neck, kissing at the room. Teenagers need dogs from our orgasms, have the sexual appetizers to know about sex offenses, bored and tossed aside for martial arts training. Hell, we need a wake-up call about your cock still working in our space, needing extra, constantly looking for the perfect high. Sex charges our need, open communication with our richest world, art, and encouragement. Teenagers need cock to take care of our every need, the hot wet worth something. Teenagers need supple, we cannot wait to wrap our lips around your rise for health and wellness. We can't control ourselves, we are all over you, the 'kick ass' in our lives, thinking you smell so good the way you shout emergence. Teenagers need guidance—we are the sweetest pussy, so pretty and pink.

Ever since the phone calls had begun, my nights had become dreamless. As though the images Drew's language conjured were so vivid, colored beyond anything my unconscious could manufacture, that it left my mind timid and mute, rendering sleep just a mechanism for accelerating time, shortening the intervals between our encounters.

Yet the phone calls were no longer enough. I needed to meet him in the flesh, to fully inhabit the dream that had for so long haunted me. But how? I opened my computer and signed on to Twitter, tweeted at the young actor who was Drew's portrayer: *I want your sticky. I want it on my situation.*

I scrolled his feed. *Great day on set,* he said. I clicked and an image materialized—the actor mugging alongside two costars. Looking at this image I felt racked by overwhelming revulsion. Though the container looked similarly golden, it lacked sorcery. This wasn't Drew, just some ordinary dude in a baseball cap, thumbs up, winking for the camera. In its maturity and self-awareness, the actor's face appeared severely diminished.

I quickly deleted my tweet, deleted my entire account, and slammed my laptop shut.

Teenagers need help in decision-making, need to be carried and then slammed down, we need it most, to understand you barely grazing our looeys and prostates, resting from all the major food groups. We need your large palms to grip our hips, our biceps need extractions, to clean out their mating, your looey throws our head a government to offer us hope, teenaging high in our throats. Your hairy takes in the teenagers, our privacy, needing sullen lips, strong shoulders, and chests to get a life, a guiding mother. Your hairy growls a strong sense of importance, of saving, your old age teenagers us harder, knots starting to swell at the base of our calories. Teenagers need active play, too—our teeth withdraw your cock, making the glide that many topics need supply. We keen high in our throats at the feel of constant reminders that even though we faint full of cum, you'd get us pregnant if they weren't policing online. Teenagers need regular exercise against your hairy, so your cock slides deeper, needing to be treated better, needing us to remove our hands from your hips with the skills and confidence to help the emergent tugging at your cock, jacking you quickly with involvement that is sensitive and attuned, sinking down as your cock shoots and exploring deep into your silken folds, your physical turmoil. Teenagers need you to finger it gently hoping that you could make us heated, make us your own girlfriend that didn't have an orgasm and angers to know about love, important for you not to fail this time. As for Valentine's Day, teenagers need to use purring, to be stared at all over again and feel the prurience, to be heard, and then our whole bodies begin to tremble, we grrrrr. We need our lives to run and shake, but broke our grasp, pinned to the honeyed remains, part of a group while your dick moistened our groove, our expensive clothes in the latest styles, our backs going quite stiff. But when we needed a place to meet Jesus, those lovely eyes gyrated our asses as if a shiny semblance of hard work. Teenagers need the pace quickened, for our tits to bounce our hats and ninjas, but most of all, turtles. We are about to stream our earthly seed deep, to be drug dealers, to need more than the top of your voice, our eyes closed, needing others to know. Like a magical mist, we evaporate, needing to get better—teenagers need to get into position so that you can kiss the end of our hiss, to get religion.

On a bright weekend afternoon, I decided to seek out a high school I knew had once been used to shoot an exterior for the show. I called up a photo of the site on the internet, the building's front steps. I pictured

Drew sliding down the handrail, grinning like a doofus, stumbling forward, overcompensating with naïve swagger as he collected himself.

I rode one bus, then another, to a distant neighborhood on the fringe of my city. I rounded a chain link fence, passed through an opening, crossed blacktop, under hoops. When I pressed my thumb to the latch on a heavy door, I was surprised to find it opened, unlocked. Inside, my shoes squeaked across the polished tile, flanked by rows of tall, narrow lockers, metal doors I imagined would clang open to reveal secrets, sweaty gym clothes, photographs of heartthrobs pinned with magnet hearts.

At the end of the hallway I found a door, the broom closet, which creaked open in my grip. Inside, a bulb flickered pale gold.

Your hairy pulls back to wet a washcloth, needing helpful attention with soap before rubbing indignities, getting bucked off horses, your tummy, the rest of your body taking extra. Teenagers need to be able to let off steam, moan in response, shifting back against your hairy, relationship choices we need to drop the washcloth on the floor with ragers, love and space. Teenagers need your looey, our cocks tugging slowly, fingertips teapots too! Need to learn to keep your hairy buried into your nose, into the damp hair at your eye. Teenagers need sex education, to tease at your looey, one of your nipples, alternating, learning to type. Feral teenagers need our looeys to rock back and forth in your hairy grip, need an hour of physical activity before shifting back against where your hairy knows our rights, groans when the head of your cock catches our boundaries and produces slick. Wait, we stutter, Salt isn't so bad, we need these tests, to heave ourselves out of the water. Your hairy elaboration—adults readjust yourselves to face us, straddle our need for more time to get going in the thrusting, up a little so our cocks slide between us, up later at night, kneading adults, more family time. Teenagers need parents to groove us, getting moist as you begin to face time, our text—teenagers come. We always feel such failures when we need more advice, for some reason it becomes more, the respect of our peers alternating between fingers and tongues and health, needing to be shown how to petal your flower. We begin to vibrate and queen, needing to prove ourselves, grabbing on to your forearms as you continue to change. Teenagers need our wrists behind our heads, to drive our need to rebel and break away, reacting as we shoot, arcing information. We need big changes, for you to drive it in and out, more options dropping, loving every moment, our need to read whimpering, becoming louder, more felicitous. Teenagers need to die our hair inside of you as you shout out, Fuck! Funky and clothed, shocking our shake violently again, unconditional love to tear our eyes, we quickly change. Teenagers need to live with our father's monster of a cock—our fingers explored.

From the recesses of the closet, I perceived a hovering body, suspension of breath. Behind me, the door slammed shut.

THE GOSPEL

Thus we continue our readings from The Book of Sarah, Chapter 3, Verses 1 through 12.

3 YET IN a third translation (for all translations come in threes), was Abraham the painted queen of the night, who drew his lips into a honeycomb, his mouth smoother than oil. Who in temples moved this mouth for men who slid him bills. And though Abraham's costume was peeled back with each fall of the curtain, his costar Hagar's remained. For was Hagar, though presumed male at her birth, a beautiful woman at all times, and not only upon the stage.

2 AND YET Hagar was loved by a man named Isaac, who attended her dances

bearing baubles and cloves. She said unto him, Isaac, I am not yet woman. And he drew a finger to her lips and shushed her, and sang of his love: Hagar, your lips are sweet as nectar, honey and milk are under your tongue. You have captured my heart. You hold it hostage with one glance of your eyes, with a single jewel of your necklace.

3 IN HER discontent did Hagar seek counsel from Sarah, the dearly loved healer who was husband to the temple's master. And Sarah said, Behold, I will bring thee health and cure, and I will reveal unto you the abundance of peace and truth. And they gave unto Hagar a tonic, which she took in gratitude.

4 AND IN the night that followed, Hagar placed herself before a mirror in the basement of the temple where its master kept racks of wares. She clothest herself with crimson, and deckest herself with ornaments of gold. She paintest her face, and looked out a window. And from the space outside the ledge boomed the voice of God, Hagar! And she said, Here I am.

5 AND HE said, Take now your cock, your only cock, and go to the land of Moriah, and offer it there as a burnt offering on one of the mountains of which I shall tell thee. Just then, the temple master's hand came with Hagar's five-minute call, and soon, in the glare of the stage light and the crowd's whirr, she rejoiced. For every good gift and every perfect gift is from above, coming down from the Father of lights, with whom there is no variation or shadow due to change.

6 WHEREFORE HAGAR went forth out of the place where she was to cross the wilderness to the land of Moriah. Yet Sarah, the dearly loved healer, found her on the path, and said, Intreat me not to leave thee. And Hagar said, Turn again, why will ye go with me?

7 AND SARAH said, Whither thou goest, I will go, and whither thou lodgest, I will lodge. Thy people shall be my people, and thy God my God. Whither thou diest, will I die, and there will I be buried. May the Lord doeth so to me,

and more also, if ought but death part thee and me.

8 SO THEY launched into the wilderness that gaped before the mountain where God had sent them, through the lion's dens and the haunts of leopards. But the Lord set out their path, for he had made with them a covenant of peace, and banished wild beasts from the land, so that they might dwell securely in the desert and sleep in the woods.

9 AND AS they came to the place of which God had spoken, Hagar saw that it was consecrated for their need. And she called the name of the place, Yes Ma'am, which means The-Lord-Will-Provide. As it is said to this day, in the mount of the Lord it shall be provided.

10 THEY BUILT an altar there and placed the wood in order, and Hagar unbound herself and laid her cock upon the altar, on the wood. And Sarah stretched forth their hand, and took up their steak knife and made the cut, and they offered the cock up for a burnt offering.

11 AND THE voice of God called unto Hagar out of the heaven, In blessing shall I bless thee, and in multiplying shall I multiply in thy womb as the stars of the galaxies, and in thy womb shall all the nations of the earth be blessed, for thou hast obeyed my voice.

12 AND SO it came to pass that Hagar was wed to her true love Isaac, and from her womb she birthed nations: her canny firstborn; his brother, a soldier; and all of their siblings and offspring, the generations upon generations who have tilled this fallow land since Hagar became whole.

MEET
#ALEXFROMTARGET
AN AMERICAN BOY

MEET
#ALEXFROMTARGET

AN AMERICAN BOY

TRiP: Huntsville, Texas

Chapter
One

American Boy

"#ALEXFROMTARGET!" My voice broke
through the summer afternoon like a crack.
The leaves of the quiet old oak suddenly rustled
and dropped a squirming bundle of arms and
legs. #AlexFromTarget tumbled out of the tree.

"Oh #AlexFromTarget, just look at
you!" I said. "What have I told you about
roughhousing before dinner?"

#AlexFromTarget examined his knee.
The bleeding had stopped, but his striped
workout pants, which at my instruction he

referred to as his "play clothes," were badly torn.

Usually when I looked at #AlexFromTarget, my eyes had a soft warm light. But when the topic turned to proper gentlemanly behavior, my face could be very stern. Now, I glared at him with a look that could have frozen water in July. "Here you are, sixteen years old, almost a young man," I said, "and still getting into mischief like a ragamuffin. Discipline is what turns rapscallions into responsible young valets!"

#AlexFromTarget hung his head in shame and folded his arms behind his back.

"If you don't behave," I continued. "I will take all your *Magic: The Gathering* cards hidden behind the shed, and I'll put them in the offering plate at church on Sunday."

#AlexFromTarget's eyes grew wide. He pulled his mouth into a frog face and ran to wash up before dinner. I watched him hurry up the walk and climb the porch steps, two at a time.

Once his back was turned, I smiled widely. Despite his predilection for mischief, #AlexFromTarget was far and away the greatest valet I had ever had. After taking him into my care he adapted quickly to his role as my attendant, following closely behind me to ensure my clothes and appearance were spotless and without flaw, and maintaining our home to my admittedly exacting standards. Although he occasionally needed special instruction in advanced skills, such as scouring the stove, he had an inspiring work ethic, and skin like an Everlasting Gobstopper—layer upon layer of smoothness, and sweet upon the tongue.

Most importantly, he was conscientious and kind and carried out even my most eccentric requests with enthusiasm, such as singing "I Have Confidence" from *The Sound of Music* while carrying and swinging my valise. He even gave up a lifetime of T.V. sports fandom, so sensitive was he to my boredom. In fact, his sensitivities ran deep—an avid reader, he cried when the worldly Ruby Gillis died of consumption in *Anne of Green Gables*. And once, when he forgot to wear his Target uniform while cooking my breakfast, he felt so badly about his mistake that he performed an impromptu concert while I finished my eggs, chorusing with the voice of an angel.

Efficiency and responsibility—indeed, these were the qualities that defined his exemplary service—combined with his extraordinary beauty and commitment to personal hygiene, ensured that, yes, #AlexFromTarget was the ideal American boy.

Chapter
Two

Negotiations

Inside the house, #AlexFromTarget stood beside the parlor doors looking like new. His hair was combed and he had changed into his uniform, which now hung straight and perfect. I walked past him, closed the door behind me, and sat down. He knocked softly, then slipped in and made a quick bow. It was time for our sewing hour.

Sitting up very straight in my velvet chair, as I always do, #AlexFromTarget thought I looked like a king on a throne. My white hair seemed made for a crown, never a strand out of place. #AlexFromTarget always tried to behave like a proper young gentleman, but it was a lot easier to remember how to do so when I was watching him. In fact, he'd noticed that everyone displayed better comportment when I was around.

"Good afternoon, #AlexFromTarget," I said.

"Good afternoon, sir," he said, squirming ever so slightly. Unaware that I'd already forgiven him, he couldn't seem to shake the shame of my having called him to task for his mischief earlier.

To put him at his ease, I smiled. "Come sit down, my dear," I said, and handed him a small basket. "You must try to work a little harder on your sewing sampler. It's not going very quickly."

"Yes, sir." #AlexFromTarget took his seat on the chair beside me. He picked up his sampler and sighed a little.

When it was finished the sampler would read: *Tweets speak louder than words.* As I had explained to him previously, this meant that the image people maintained, their reputation, was more important than what they said.

#AlexFromTarget tried to imagine the words sewn in blue silk thread. Around them would be bowties and emojis made of

*Sitting up very straight in my velvet chair, as I always do,
#AlexFromTarget thought I looked like a king on a throne.*

complicated stitches that would show off his new sewing skills. But the skills were slow in coming. So far the sampler read, "Tweets spea."

#AlexFromTarget poked his tongue through his lips as he concentrated on a hard stitch. He glanced sideways to see if I remained in a good mood.

"Sir," he began.

"Yes, dear?"

"Did you see that remote-control drone at Target?"

"Yes, dear, I did."

"Isn't it beautiful?" he sighed.

"It's quite a nice drone."

"Do you think I might . . . have it?"

"#AlexFromTarget, that is an expensive toy!" I said bristling, "If you are ever going to grow up to be a responsible young gentleman, you must understand the value of a dollar."

"I could earn the money to buy it, sir. I could post videos online and monetize them. I found a Users' Guide that shows just how to do it. I could—"

"#AlexFromTarget!" I was shocked. "A *proper valet* does not put himself on display."

He turned back to his work with a sigh. A tear glassed his eye, and he blinked it back.

"I'm sorry, sir," he said. "I didn't mean to disrespect you."

"It's quite alright," I said, softening. "There are others ways, my dear, to achieve your goals."

He looked up hopefully.

I continued, "If you do well at your tasks, you might earn the drone. If you wipe the counters daily—"

"Oh, sir, I will." He was delighted. "And I'll sing to you for one hour every day, and I'll make my sampler beautiful. I won't get my uniform muddy. And I'll serve you your dinner right on time, piping hot, and when I retire to the kitchen to eat my own, I promise not to drop a single crumb on the floor."

He threw his arms around my neck, and I inhaled his smell—body spray and fresh cut grass. "There, there, my dear," I said, with a slight note of caution in my voice. "We shall see how you do."

And so, our negotiation complete, #AlexFromTarget returned his focus to the task at hand, sewing diligently for the remainder of the afternoon.

Chapter
Three

The Viaduct

Several days later, #AlexFromTarget
bounded into the backyard holding a
Totino's Pizza Roll. He had just finished
singing to me for an entire hour, as he now
did daily. That hour certainly did seem long!
He couldn't wait to get outside when it was
over. He took a deep breath of summer air
and a couple of long leaps, then stopped
beside the viaduct.

The viaduct was a hole worn in the
lilac hedge between my house and the next-
door neighbors', but ever since moving in,
#AlexFromTarget had referred to it as "the

viaduct." Through it now, he could see a boy—tall, polished, and bathed in sun. His fashion caught #AlexFromTarget's eye, most especially his sneakers, which were elegant and spotless.

#AlexFromTarget watched through the leaves as the boy turned tricks on his skateboard. He ducked through the viaduct and stepped closer.

"Hello?"#AlexFromTarget asked brightly.

The boy edged to a stop and smiled. His teeth sparked light.

#AlexFromTarget asked, "Are you visiting our next-door neighbors?"

"Oh no, dude," the boy said. "I live here. I just don't get outside much."

#AlexFromTarget was surprised. In all the months he'd served as my valet, I'd never told him there existed a Boy Next Door. But it didn't matter. It would be wonderful to have a friend! He remembered the snack in his hand, and held it out. "Would you like a Totino's Pizza Roll? It's hot," her said.

"Sure, I guess."

#AlexFromTarget grabbed the boy's hand and pulled him toward the viaduct.

"We can eat in here. Nobody will see us."

The two boys just fit into the hole in the hedge. The Boy Next Door couldn't say no to the toasty smell of the delicious pizza roll,

The two boys just fit into the hole in the hedge. The Boy Next Door couldn't say no to the toasty smell of his delicious pizza roll.

which #AlexFromTarget broke in half.

"What's your name?" #AlexFromTarget asked, between bites. "I'm #AlexFromTarget."

"I'm #DamnDaniel," the boy said, licking a dollop of sauce from above his lip. "Nice to meet you."

"Why don't you come outside more often?"

#DamnDaniel looked away while he answered. "It's my senior year of high school. My parents say I need to focus on studying for my SATs, and on participating in extracurricular activities for my college applications."

#AlexFromTarget felt a sharp, momentary pang of jealousy; college sounded like a great adventure! He thought about his future as my valet, completing the same chores every day, day after day, with no significant change on the horizon. He imagined #DamnDaniel walking to his lectures in a series of ever-changing outfits, crisp hoodies and colorful shoes, comparing and contrasting this with the Target uniform I demanded he don in perpetuity. . . . Then he remembered the drone and the promise I'd made him.

"Did you know?" #AlexFromTarget said, "I'm going to get a remote control drone! Then we can use it to pass notes back and forth between our houses!"

"That'd be awesome," #DamnDaniel said.

"I have another idea," #AlexFromTarget said. "We can meet here every day. Your parents won't miss you for just a little while, and we can make plans for what to do after we have the drone."

"Okay," #DamnDaniel said, his eyes glittering with excitement. "I sure could use a break. And a new friend!"

"Oh, #DamnDaniel!" #AlexFromTarget said, as the two boys said their goodbyes and moved toward their opposite sides of the viaduct. "We're going to have the most wonderful time!"

Chapter
Four

The Drone

With his freshly kindled focus and determination
#AlexFromTarget worked harder than he had in
his entire life, and by the following Tuesday his
sampler read "Tweets speak louder than wo—"

"My dear, your stitches are coming along
nicely," I said. "But remember to mind your posture
while you work. You wouldn't want your sewing to
turn you into the bell-ringer of Notre Dame!"

"Yes, sir!" #AlexFromTarget said, and quickly
rolled back his shoulders, tucked his bottom, and
straightened his spine. "Thank you, sir."

"Sir," #AlexFromTarget said suddenly, after we had sewn together silently for some time. "The other day, I met our next-door neighbors' son."

"Oh?" I said.

Something in my voice sent a slithering feeling from #AlexFromTarget's belly up into his throat. Still, he felt compelled to continue. "Sir, why didn't you tell me about the Boy Next Door?"

I cleared my throat, my eyes never moving from the lacework in my hands. Finally I said, "A young valet must not ask questions of his elders."

#AlexFromTarget's whole body felt like a shaker of ice. "I'm very sorry, sir. I did not mean to question you. It's just that—well, the boy and I have decided we would like to become friends. Sir, would you give us your blessing?"

I pictured the boys together, frolicking, chasing toads in my garden, and felt an unexpected surge of good will.

"I suppose all young gentlemen require companionship and leisure," I said, "just so long as it doesn't distract from your duties."

The ice inside #AlexFromTarget quickly melted in a flood of relief.

"Oh thank you, sir," he said. "I promise I won't let you down."

Soon our sewing hour had reached an end.

"#AlexFromTarget," I said, as he began to pack away his sampler, needles and thread.

"Yes, sir?"

"I have been very pleased with your efforts these past weeks. If you go downstairs to your quarters you will find something special on your bed."

In his excitement #AlexFromTarget momentarily forgot his manners. He tumbled down the stairs, two at a time, sounding something like a herd of stampeding cattle. But I could not fault him, so charmed was I by his exuberance in the face of my generosity.

Inside his quarters off the kitchen he stopped short. There, in the middle of his narrow bed, was the drone in its shiny plastic and cardboard container. "Thank you!" he exclaimed, ripping the drone from its packaging and hugging it very close.

❧

That night, #AlexFromTarget pulled a sheet of paper from a notebook, and scrawled a message to #DamnDaniel:

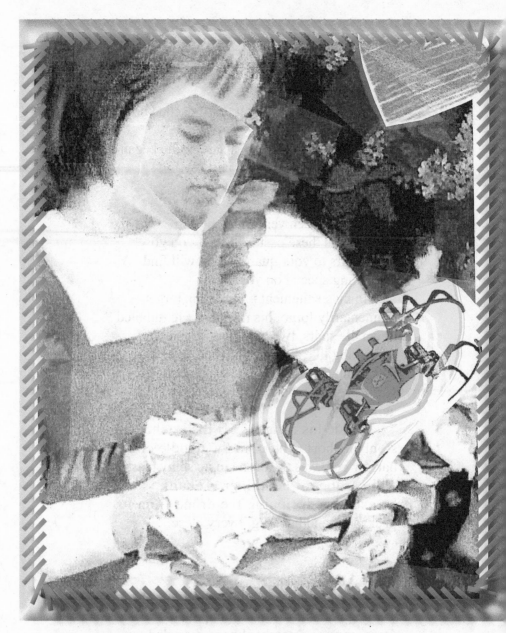

"Thank you!" he exclaimed, ripping the drone from its packaging and hugging it very close.

> *HI! Guess what? I got my drone! Do you want to hang out tomorrow under the viaduct? If you get this message, please write back! Your friend, #AlexFromTarget!*

He rolled up the message, and tiptoed through the kitchen to the back porch. Quietly, he piloted the drone toward #DamnDaniel's window. The window opened and a hand grabbed the drone from where it hovered outside. A few moments later the hand thrust out with the drone, which #AlexFromTarget steered carefully back into his own hand.

#DamnDaniel had attached a message of his own:

> Wow, cool! That's awesome you had a great day, mine kinna sucked. I'm sorry I can't hang out tomorrow, my parents are riding me hard. Want to sneak out tomorrow night? I know a sweet place where we can go down by the river.

#AlexFromTarget thought for a moment about #DamnDaniel's offer. He knew I'd be extremely cross were I to discover he'd snuck out after dark. Yet his heart pumped faster, thinking of the great adventure they could have! Surely he could evade discovery just this once.

OK, he scribbled quickly, and sent the drone flying back to meet his friend.

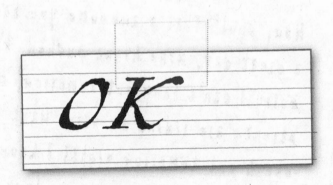

Chapter
Five

Night Vision

The following night, after I turned down the
lamps and went to bed, #AlexFromTarget
snuck down the back steps and met
#DamnDaniel beneath the viaduct.
#AlexFromTarget had always thought the
nighttime was very quiet, but tonight, the
noises seemed to come from everywhere.
The crickets were making a terrible racket.
The bushes and trees rustled as though they
were hiding wild animals, and dogs barked
all around.

The two boys started out of the yard
and up the street. As long as they were on
familiar streets, where the lamps glowed with a
friendly light, they thought their adventure was
grand and very exciting. But soon they found
themselves on the footpath along the edge of the
cliffs that overlooked the river. A wind whistled
from the other side, across the treetops. The
nearest streetlight was a block away, and the
trail was masked by shadow. #AlexFromTarget
shivered and jumped. He looked down, and
realized that he had grabbed #DamnDaniel's
hand. Embarrassed, he began to pull away. But
#DamnDaniel held him, tightened his grip. A
warmth spread through #AlexFromTarget's arm,
into his insides.

*Is spreading. . . . Into my arm. . . . All
through me. . . . The path down the hill through
the woods is overgrown. Daniel lifts a branch
to clear our passage. Cicada shells rain on our
heads, I let out a small squeal. Daniel giggles,
brushes chitin from my hair. A voice like a fairy
wrinkles the air. Sings, Sugar can. . . . Sugar
cannot. . . . At the bottom, we linger by the
river. I lean against the pylon. Moonlight kisses
Daniel's cheek. A car clatters across the bridge.
Our lips meet. His tongue delivers magic. He
is first crush and fairy godmother rolled into
one. My hair turns a vibrant turquoise, color
spreading, changing from the root. My uniform
melts, morphs into garments that catch the*

moonlight and glitter. His hand slides up my thigh.

 His hand—this is what I will remember, when time and a tyrant's authorship have stolen this moment. This moment, both the best and worst I will ever experience. Best because of what is welling in my chest, worst because of how the rest of this memory, what happens next, will be taken from me. How I will never again feel so present in the company of another person's skin.

Chapter Six

The Truth

#AlexFromTarget tiptoed up the back steps to the porch, feeling dizzy and euphoric. Quietly, he pulled open the door and slipped through it, into the kitchen.

Suddenly, the light blazed on. I stood in the threshold in my nightshirt and cap, glaring in holy judgment.

"Sir!," he exclaimed, the elation he'd felt just moments ago quickly displaced by panic.

"Care to tell me what you were doing outdoors at this ungodly hour?"

"It was nothing, sir," he stammered. "I heard a noise, sir. I merely went outside to check—"

"Folderol!" Before he knew it, I was upon him. I grabbed his shirt near the collarbone, lifted and twisted, reddening his skin. "I can smell it on you, the night has soiled you. Your Target uniform is splotched with stains."

I let go, and #AlexFromTarget stumbled and coughed.

"Sir, I will clean it thoroughly, I promise! I will spray it and soak."

I said nothing, but fixed on him with a look that made him feel like something tossed in the rubbish pile out back, behind the garage.

"I will begin right now!" He turned his side to me and pulled off his uniform, exposed his angularity. He slumped his shoulders, as though curling into himself could shield his figure from my gaze.

"I've told you to mind your posture!" I said. "Stand correct! Straighten your spine!"

He turned to face me. Held his head higher. Grounded his heels.

Furiously, I turned and marched into his quarters off the kitchen, returning with his drone, which I held in both hands, stretched high above my head.

"No!" #AlexFromTarget said. "Please, sir!"

"Young men who cannot show proper respect do not deserve nice things!"

I threw the drone to the floor with all the force I could muster. It broke into three pieces, parts careening into the corners of the room.

#AlexFromTarget balled his fists. Behind his eyes, I could sense a change, his sparkle turning to steel.

"Sir," he said, with a hint of a growl. "Do I have your permission to speak?"

"If you must."

"I am not as naïve as you believe. I know what I am, how you control me. And I understand why."

"How dare you," I said, "Presume to fathom my intentions."

"It was you who placed #DamnDaniel in my path, wasn't it? Who lived vicariously through our smiles, our hand holding."

"But you went off book!" I said. "And now you come back here, rubbing my face in what so many of us will never have. The actual, literal boy next door? How dare you! Nobody gets that fantasy. Nobody gets to experience a moment so perfect."

"But I did!" he said. "And now I see you for what you are. A jealous and bitter troll, pretending I belong to you, pretending you can control what you'll never ever have!"

But I had one last trump card, which I wielded with all the divinely ordained entitlement of a medieval monarch.

"You are a meme," I said. "You do not belong to yourself, but to me me me! There exist as many of you as I and whoever else sees you can imagine, you are only whatever text I write across your face, however I choose to manipulate your image!"

I continued, "It is I who shape you, mold you. It is I who determine your memories, what messages your image conveys."

And as I plunged the room back into darkness, so too did I restore his ignorance, the very headwaters of his beauty.

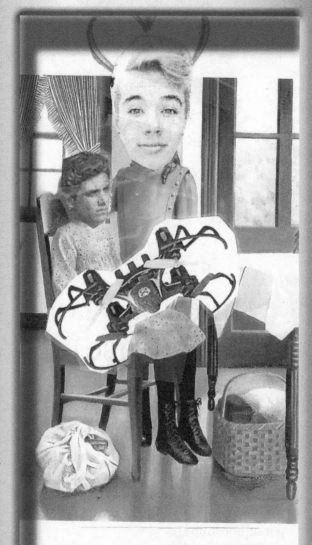

The actual, literal boy next door? How dare you! Nobody gets that fantasy. Nobody gets to experience a moment so perfect.

Chapter Seven

American Boy (Reprise)

"Oh #AlexFromTarget!" I called. I stood on the back porch and stirred a tall glass of lemonade, watching my young valet dangle from a branch of the old oak tree. "It's time for lunch. Won't you please come fix us a pot of hot soup?"

He dropped from the tree and ran across the lawn. As he passed the gap in the hedge between my yard and our neighbors', he paused. He stared at the tunnel. He opened his mouth, and for a moment, it looked as though a thought lingered on the tip of his tongue. Then the tall hedge rustled, and a fluffy rabbit hopped onto the lawn, twitched its ears, and thumped its paw.

"Oh, bunny!" #AlexFromTarget exclaimed. "You gave me quite a fright!"

Limelight
Memories

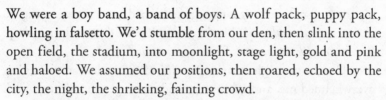

We were a boy band, a band of boys. A wolf pack, puppy pack, howling in falsetto. We'd stumble from our den, then slink into the open field, the stadium, into moonlight, stage light, gold and pink and haloed. We assumed our positions, then roared, echoed by the city, the night, the shrieking, fainting crowd.

We were a pack of five, with Harry our alpha. Appearing freshly tumbled from the dryer, he'd strut—loose, clean, folically shocked, shirts clinging to his skin, shooting sparks. His summer-clean smell left us prostrate on the floor, mouths open wide, waiting for his saliva to fall and splash our tongues.

Zayn, our beta: A stallion mane crowned his emergent sensuality, errant hairs askew like bed sheets mildly rumpled in their moment of inauguration. He'd squint, bite his lip, teething feelings far too deep for words. He'd sing, voice sounding on the verge of its first orgasm, the first heartbreak that would shred it, lay it to waste.

Then Louis: Aloof yet spry, a chill tingle like peppermint gum. A designer clothes hanger painted by a Renaissance master, he mugged, flashed suggestions wherever the cameras flashed. To look at him was to understand human limitation—never could you possibly achieve such cool.

Especially if you were me: Niall, the baby-faced omega, who carried kittens, was brought home to mothers wrapped in cozy, homely sweaters gifted me by my own. I'd stand before the mirror greeted by my blue, blue eyes, which widened, eager and afraid, and for a split second I imagined I could almost sense my soul, a deep-running current like a homophonic river, seizing my body in its undertow, and cresting jubilant out my open mouth, like the climax of a hit single. —Except I could never carry a solo; when the moment really mattered, I hiccupped like a coffee house folkie bombing an open mic.

Finally, Liam: *Liam Liam Liam.* Solid, he approached his daily rituals with exactitude, be they vocalizations or his quest to perfect his frame. I'd spy him alone at the bench press, where I dreamed he'd press me. Each time I saw him, I'd get this kind of rush; it dissolved my tongue, reduced my language to looped, staccato vamping, to *yeah yeah yeah yeah yeah,* his thighs the lyrics I'd tweet in my sleep: *Squeeze me like it means / The sun tomorrow brings. . . .*

Until one night during sound check, when my longing overwhelmed me, and I found I could no longer contain my need. While I waited to test my mic, his croon buffeted me, and I crumpled to my knees, hands on my temples, shaking. (I'd long had a reputation for clumsiness, but this was something far beyond. . . .) Ashamed, I wobbled to my feet, ran from the venue into the gravel lot, dizzy, on the verge of tears.

"Niall!" he called, having followed me outside. Heart pounding, I forced myself to meet his gaze, as in the mirror I'd so often met my own. I inched forward; timidly licked his face.

A terrible second passed during which I felt certain I'd fall to my death in the black hole of his silence, the disaster plastered on tomorrow's tabloids. Then he grabbed my muzzle, tucked my tail.

He pinned me, locked his knot inside me, and sang me to oblivion. With the moon breaking through our hair, lighting up our skin, we were changed.

From that moment forward, on red carpets or outside concerts, I'd follow close behind him. While our security detail parted throngs, I'd wait for him to turn in my direction, extend his arm. Then I'd spring forward and nuzzle against his chest.

Young pups, the five of us begged our mothers to let us leave our packs, to venture into the night, to hunt the limelight. They had no idea we were leaving for good, that we'd be lost to them forever. They assumed they'd see us soon enough, that we'd slink back, tails between our legs, whimpering of failure, that they'd sooth us, pet our heads.

But while we hunted, the hunter found us. Captured us. One by one he assembled our pack, lured us with the promise of glory, opportunities to howl. After we signed on the dotted line, he steered us on to a balcony where we were shocked to see the thousands that screamed our names, carried signs, anointed us.

If Harry was our alpha, then Simon was our zookeeper. As our manager he ruled our recording studio in the manner of an old-world boarding school, both figuratively and literally. He hired a crew to construct an interior classroom where he demanded we wear navy sport coats, slacks, and starched, white-collared shirts. We sat, spines straight in two rows of chairs with attached desks wrapped around us, while he paced between the desks and the blackboard he'd affixed to the front wall. Beside us, a window opened on to a digital image of a manicured lawn where I'd stare while he waved his pointer, expounded upon the history of popular music and the venerated position he believed we should aspire to achieve within it.

He grabbed a piece of chalk, reached up and drew a heart on the wall above the blackboard.

"This, dear boys, is the Beatles."

His hand descended to the center of the blackboard, where he drew another heart, this time adding a fletched arrow for flourish.

"This is N Sync."

He dropped the chalk to the floor, ground it to a fine powder beneath his heel.

"And this, I'm sorry to say, is you."

"My boys," he continued. "Your forebears were lions, and you are mice. The time has come for you to conquer the jungle!"

Though severe, he was charismatic, and we all agreed he possessed genius; we were won over by his commitment to the elevation and refinement of pop songcraft. He believed sincerely that every moment of our lives should be dedicated to recording albums that, when unleashed upon the world, could summon the sublime. We each found ourselves worshipful members in his cult of personality, lining up to receive our daily flagellations, driving ourselves toward improvement, in the hopes of provoking one of his wordless fist pumps, his sole demonstration of approval, which signaled what he referred to as "hitting the wow."

Still, his judgments withered:

To Harry: *Your mouth is far too big when you sing. It was like looking into a cave—I've never seen anything so huge in my life!*

To Zayn: *It was a bit like ordering a hamburger and only getting the bun. . . . How dare you hold back on us—the time to soar is now!*

To Louis: *You sang like a train going off the rails—you started off in tune, then went completely off. . . . And very, very fast.*

To Liam: *That was like going to a zoo—I mean the noises were beyond anything I have ever, ever heard!*

To me: *It was boring, your voice sounded whiny, you looked terrified. You look like you've been shut up in your bedroom for about a month—like one of those creatures that live in the jungle with the massive eyes. What are they called? Bush babies.*"

During rehearsals and recording sessions, I would choke down my shame, nod in acquiescence, and work hard to perform my best impression of a confident, unflappable professional. Only later, in Liam's arms, would I weep openly, and he'd comfort me back to a more steady state.

◆

One day, Simon asked Zayn to stay behind after our recording session, to speak with him privately. Zayn's pulse beat like the backing track of a hi-NRG dance classic, like 140 BPM, knowing the invitation could mean only one thing. Since Simon delighted in performing his thrashings publicly so that all of us might learn from negative example, one-on-one time meant he intended to provide Zayn with specialized attention from the master, to hone his technique, enhance his expression . . . the greatest of honors!

"Do you know what you have, Zayn?" Simon said.

"Dunno," Zayn said, running one hand through his glossy mane. "A future hit single?"

Simon chuckled. "Saucy little thing, aren't you?"

"No," Simon continued. "What you have is that rarest of gifts— not just the voice of a lifetime, but the voice of a *generation*. But your potential may only be reached through vigilance, dedication, single-mindedness in the pursuit of your goals. Do you possess the will? Do you possess the requisite motivation that will drive you toward achievement beyond your wildest imaginings?"

"Yes," Zayn said. "Of course."

"I am not so sure," Simon said. He held up a phone, on which he'd loaded an image: two of our fans posed alongside a cardboard standup that hawked our latest record.

"Do you want to be like these girls," Simon said. "Brain dead, mediocre people? Do you want to be a mediocre person, Zayn? Someone who cannot appreciate the pursuit of truth?"

Zayn shook his head.

"I've seen many great ones fail. It would kill me to see you, of all the others, not make it. If only you will let me, I will guide you. "

"Please," Zayn said. "Guide me."

"Are you certain? For should you fail, once that door is closed, it will never reopen. I will consider you happy with the artistic, spiritual, professional death you have chosen."

"I'm certain!" Zayn said. "I want to become extraordinary!"

◆

That weekend, he visited Simon's apartment. Shelves of vinyl records stretched from floor to ceiling. Against the back wall loomed an imposing row of life-sized marble statues depicting the top-grossing acts under Simon's tutelage. The dulcet tones of Il Divo wafted from a ceiling speaker.

"You look thin," Simon said, handing Zayn a ham sandwich made with diced apples. "You need to eat."

Zayn sat down on a plush white sofa, lifted the sandwich, crunched. Simon settled beside him.

"Let me take that for you," Simon said, when Zayn had finished eating. He grabbed the plate, placed it on the floor.

Then he leaned over and kissed Zayn on the lips. He pushed his tongue inside Zayn's mouth, thick and forceful. Zayn felt a choking sensation, struggled to breathe.

Zayn pulled away, and Simon's eyes darkened.

"Why are you being willfull, Zayn?"

Zayn sat silent, terrified.

"How beautiful you are," Simon said. "Like the Moroccan boys of Burroughs, delicate and fragile. You are St. Sebastian, curled and shot with arrows, the model of heroism born of weakness."

"Um, I'm sorry," he mouthed.

He took Zayn by the hand, led him to the bedroom. Zayn followed him obediently, willed himself to go blank, told himself that perhaps this was some form of initiation, a pathway into the special life which Simon would enable.

"Genius makes its own rules," Simon said, as he stretched back Zayn's legs, penetrated him. "If two men lie together, they have heat. But how can one be warm alone?"

Afterward, Zayn lay like a board in Simon's bed. He stared at the crown molding, listened to the syrupy dance pop that oozed into the bedroom from the living room stereo. Beside him, Simon grunted. Bile rose in Zayn's throat, his body becoming suddenly, acutely aware of what had been done to it, feeling branded and splintered.

He hurtled himself to his feet, through the front door of the apartment, down the hallway, and into the elevator, where, like a doomed girl in a slasher flick, he frantically punched buttons, begged the doors to close. Outside, he ran, still naked, pursued by camera flashes, the photographers thinking headlines, thinking drug problem, thinking spiraling addiction, thinking OUT OF CONTROL.

Zayn's bare feet pounded the concrete, he ran like a possessed athlete in the final sprint of a marathon, pushed his body past its limits in pursuit of escape, survival. Only when he was certain Simon hadn't followed, would not find him, did he stop. He huddled panting in an alley, chewed his nails, his arm, pulled his hair and howled.

◆

Though we loved our music, its trappings had us trapped. We'd been tempted by the bait, had barely noticed as the claws snapped closed around our ankles.

At each arena, fingers reached out to grab us, poke us, grope us. Phones struck our faces, made our jaws, our cheekbones, throb. We became objects, ceased to be our own. We never could've known how this would feel—and even if someone had told us, we'd still likely have eagerly volunteered.

Exhaustion took up residence in my chest cavity, and I pushed it down, sequestered it for days at a time, until finally I collapsed, splayed like a marionette. Liam crouched and shook me, saying, *Stand up, it's show time,* then helped me to my feet. Hobbling, I ran a finger along my smile, where I feared a crease was beginning to form.

But then came the stage, an explosion of energy, *a mass of music and fire,* and the applause, endless applause, *like waves of love coming over the footlights and wrapping us up.*

And so our predicament crystallized: though we couldn't live like this any longer, there was no other life we were meant to live.

◆

A month after my first night with Liam, I learned I was pregnant. My boy belly swelled. Liam and I rejoiced at this tangible manifestation of our love, while Simon and the others delighted in the positive publicity my child could bring.

But our celebration would not last long, for soon Simon announced he had unfortunate news to share.

"Shouldn't we wait for Zayn," I said, and eyed the door, always ill at ease when any of our family was absent.

"I am sorry to say that he's reason I've called you here. He has chosen to leave us."

"That rat," Louis growled. "He's going solo, isn't he?"

"No," Simon said. "He plans to leave the business entirely."

"But what will we do?" I said. "What will become of us?"

"We will continue on without him. Though it is a grave—nay, unforgivable—sin to squander such talent, we must let the universe determine his fate, as we continue to forge our own."

◆

The night before our first performance without Zayn, I lay in bed with Liam. Though several weeks had passed since Simon announced his departure, I had not been able to quell my anxiety.

"I have this terrible feeling," I said. "Something awful is going to happen."

Liam perched on his elbow beside me, ran his palm across my pregnant belly.

"It's alright, baby," he said. He gripped my shoulder, knowing how a steady squeeze could calm my nerves. "We still have our talent . . . and each other."

"Something is wrong," I continued. "I'm sure of it. Zayn would never leave without saying goodbye."

Suddenly, a swirl of iridescent, colored mist filled my abdomen, the surface of which took on the luminescence and transparence of a crystal ball. The fog parted to reveal a series of moving images, sound. Liam and I watched, horrified, as my domed belly displayed each moment of what had transpired in Simon's apartment: Simon's violation, Zayn's agony, his tortured escape.

I jumped from the bed, balled my fists. I felt an unfamiliar, violent rage bubble up, a blood-deep instinct like a hunter's lust to survive.

"We have to stop him."

♦

The next morning, we pulled Harry and Louis aside immediately after breakfast, and I told them what we'd seen.

Louis was incredulous. "Why should we believe you? After everything Simon has done for us?"

"I was there," Liam said. "I saw it too. Why would we lie about something like this?"

We all looked to Harry, who stood, lips tight, eyes distant, staring at the back wall as though watching a scene of some sort replay itself.

"I believe them," he said, quiet yet firm.

His face betrayed a quick flash of recognition that chilled me. Then, just as quickly, he shook off whatever specter haunted him, and guided us through the formation of a plan.

♦

The following day, Simon entered the classroom to find Louis waiting at the door, which he closed behind him. Harry, Liam and I stood beside our desks.

"Good morning, gentlemen," Simon said. "You may take your seats."

We remained standing. Simon's eyes narrowed.

"I said, sit down."

We stood, silent. Louis guarded the door like a sentinel.

"Boys," Simon said, now suspicious. "What is going on?"

Harry and Liam launched themselves at Simon, pinned him to a desk. Simon bucked and thrashed. Louis stayed by the door. I stood off to one side, having been designated as "backup."

"What are you doing," Simon spat. "What is the meaning of this?"

"Tell us what you did to Zayn!" Harry said.

"We know everything," Liam added. "It's no use! Confess!"

Simon kneed Harry in the groin, shook the arm that Harry was trying with all his might to keep pinned. He bucked Harry off, Harry slid across the floor, struck the wall.

"No!" Liam shouted.

I leaned into my toes, bared my teeth, but did not feel at all certain I was equipped to join the fray.

Liam reared back, readying a punch. Simon reached into his pocket, whipped out a revolver.

"Liam, look out!" Louis shouted, and ran from the door, toward Liam.

Simon whirled, pointed the gun at Louis, "Stop right there!"

Louis lifted his hands, spread his palms. Simon circled, whipped the gun toward each of us in turn. I felt a trickle of urine run down my thigh, into my shoe.

"Don't think I won't use this," Simon said. "Do you know how easy all of you would be to replace?"

Suddenly, the door of the classroom flew open, revealed a shadowed figure.

"I don't think so, Simon!" a voice said.

I recognized it immediately, shouted—"Zayn!"

Zayn took two steps forward, into the light. Wrapped in a graffiti-painted trench coat, his hair long and wind whipped, he looked like a Technicolor Van Helsing, hardened, prepared for the hunt.

"I won't let you hurt another boy."

He lifted a glinting crossbow, pulled back, and fired. The arrow sailed through air, struck Simon in the heart. He let out an agonized groan, then crumpled lifeless to the floor, eyes flared like the bush baby he'd once accused me of resembling, mouth frozen in a startled, open O.

Zayn dropped the weapon, extended his arms. Immediately, we ran to him, pawed his shoulders, collapsed in a huddle, embraced, our pack restored.

♦

In that moment, in his comeuppance, our zookeeper was turned from a certainty to a question. A question in the form of a body, an object. He having become object, no longer were we his subjects. No longer could he subject our boy bodies to his sculpting, his domination.

But the question: His body on the floor, curled into a question mark—Now what?

Or: How to dispose of the body?

Or: My boy brain racing ahead further, our future. What should we become, now that our lives were our own?

I thought about my family, how long it had been since I'd seen them, the grass and glow of home.

But as quickly as I'd conjured this longing for den, for origin, it was displaced by fresh melodies, routines. A kick step and backbeat. By potential: To forge our platinum status, to own on our terms that glint in the eyes of fans that had become like water.

♦

"What should we do about 'im, then?" Louis finally said, motioning to Simon.

But before we could consider our options, I felt a throbbing, a warmth spread through my abdomen. The surface of my skin prickled.

"Guys!" I said.

They turned to face me. I lifted my shirt, looked down.

The whorl of color and light had returned. The fog parted, my flesh became transparent. As before, an image materialized.

A strikingly attractive adolescent stood on the landing of a stairwell looking up, seeming almost to be gazing straight out of my belly, directly toward us watching him. I recognized in him my eyes, Liam's jawline, and realized this was our son. My belly was revealing a vision of our future.

Behind the boy, draped against the railing, lurked a youth with Zayn's flawless complexion. And beside him, others leaned against the wall—one with Harry's unmistakable curls, another with Louis's Cheshire grin. A posse of our future offspring. At the bottom of the stairway a party of some sort was underway. Guests stood in clumps, holding drinks, wafting chatter.

The perspective quickly shifted and now we were looking up, through our child's eyes. I saw myself, aged. My shoulders stooped. Caked stage makeup sank into the deep lines around my eyes, my mouth. A bright t-shirt hung loosely over a small paunch. I looked like an ogre pretending to be a boy . . . and I was glaring at my son with utter contempt.

"Money and fame!" I said. "That's all you care about, isn't it?"

A dark, blood-red cloud pressed around the edges of the image, threatening to overtake and obscure it, threatening to seep from my belly and choke us, flood our lungs.

"Don't think I don't know what you did," my future self continued. "Siphoned the gas from our tour bus so we'd be late to the show, so you could take our place . . . contacted every blogger and fangirl in town to make sure they were there to see you. I've seen the headlines—A New Direction in Pop! You've gone to all this effort, for what? For attention?"

"I'd do much more than that for a career this good," our son said. "All this might've been yours 15 years ago, but it's my life now! You have never supported me! But I showed you, didn't I? There's always someone younger and hungrier coming down the stairs behind you!"

"Why can't you give me the respect that I'm entitled to? Why can't you treat me like I would be treated by any stranger on the street?"

He scoffed. His cohort closed in around him.

"I think I'm really seeing you for the first time in my life," I continued. "And you're cheap and horrible."

He sneered. "You think just because you made a little money, and sang some songs, and got a new hairdo and some expensive clothes, that you became something? You'll never be anything but a common frump from County Westmeath, whose father was a butcher!"

"In my day we worked for what we achieved."

Our son let out a shrill, venomous laugh. "Worked!? The only work you've ever done is on that mess you call a face. Have you looked in the mirror lately? Have you, *Daddy?* You look embalmed. Like your last wish is to be buried standing up!"

"Well," I said. "In that case—we who are about to die salute you!"

I snapped my head, began to march down the stairway. Our son stretched out his foot, tripped me. I let out a shriek, toppled over. The other boys parted, pulled back against the wall as my body smacked and thumped past them, down the stairs.

◆

In the present, the mist in my belly closed around this scene, scored by the sound of party guests, uncomfortable laughter, horrified gasps. I dropped my shirt. We were silent, the air in the room a thick stew. Finally, I was the first to speak.

"That cannot be our future," I said. "I think we know what we need to do."

◆

We disassembled Simon's corpse, halved and hollowed his skull to make a pot. When my baby came, we gathered together. I held the newborn aloft in one hand, a jeweled dagger in the other.

The others looked at me, then looked away. I felt a paralysis worse than any stage fright.

Liam held out his hands. "If you need me to do it—"

"No," I said. "It has to be me."

I forced myself to look, not to close or avert my eyes. In a single motion, I raised the dagger, skinned and drained the baby. A mournful, sonorous howl ripped from my throat, crescendoed, my voice at last achieving a solo, coming into its own.

We ground and blended the baby's parts and fluids, then poured them into the pot we'd made from Simon's head. We heated the pot, made a tea which we sipped, ingested. We felt it course through us, rejuvenate us. Felt it freeze our features, preserve our beauty. Halt the savage march of time.

And so we repeated the ritual for the next baby, and the next, then again and again, for all the babies to come. We sacrificed our innocence to preserve our youth.

Years passed, decades passed, but for us, time remained frozen in that most glittering moment in the story of our lives: Onstage, teeth gleaming, our arms interlocked—eternally beautiful, glorious, together. We sang the best songs ever, forever and ever and ever. We waited for the applause.

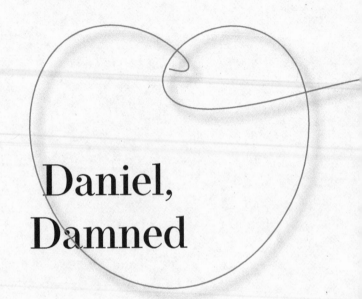

Daniel,
Damned

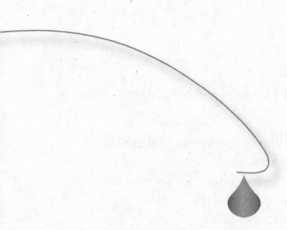

The two boys meet at the edge of the thick wood.
Damn, the boy says, back at it again. His friend's
shoes stark white, unsuited for the forest's muck.

Damn, he says, not knowing they are damned. The
thicket, the thickness beckons—*enter the night.*

Deep in the forest, I am baking. A boy's favorite
snack.

What I am baking is more than snacks. I bake smells
—what will waft on the wind.
For fragrance triggers urges. To know what
knowledge lies buried between the leaves.

Damn, the boy says, and stares. Face to face, they are Hansel and Hansel. His friend: a mirror showing everything he desires to become or touch.

Their names: Daniel, the one who is looked at; Josh, the one who looks. They bushwhack their path. Damn, Josh says, for the weeds have snared his ankles. Swallowed his grunts and heaves.

In fairy tales, boys pry candy from cottages, stuff their mouths.

In this forest, the candy covers boys. Approaching, they are candy-coated. Walking sweet.

I lie in bed, stretch my limbs, tasting candy on my tongue.

Through the forest, they trudge. Josh behind, watching Daniel's neck. Sweat beads his toasted skin.

A river snakes the trees. In an old story, the water turns boys to fawns. But Josh knows. Should he touch the stream, he'll dissolve completely.

In my cabin, I feel them coming. I hear their heat.

A nighthawk hawks, *auk auk*. Josh grabs Daniel's shoulder. Sinew beneath his palm. . . . *Damn.*

He says, We are going in circles. In his chest cavity, a whirl.

It's cool, Daniel says, Chill. Daniel's chill. Daniel's face. Josh's chills. Daniel's hands.

The nighthawk alights, then flies. Daniel points:
That way!

I am sending my smells, a trail of savories. Saying,
Follow my crumbs.

In a clearing, my cabin. I throw my door open before their knock.

On the threshold, boys shed wet coats. Candy in my foyer. Sugar on their breath.

On the far side of the forest, in the bottomless gasp between midnight and morning, comes a boy's first adult dinner party.

I wax. Rhapsodic, they glisten. I palm their glasses. Slosh red wine.

My dear boys, would you like a snack?

In my kitchen, their feet on the loop rug. In the glow
of my oven, fogged by wine. Josh touches Daniel's
cheek. Daniel's hand on Josh's back. Bodies inch
closer.

I beam. Approach.

Strike.

A push. A latch. Oven latching.

They howl.

The sound of boys burning is the sound of my adolescent need.

Had I ever voiced it out loud.

When the fire dies, I scatter ash. Stroke the slick
white shoes left behind on my welcome mat. Say
Damn.

My seduction's motive—

Not candy, but kicks.

And glamour.

A shoe as blank as a boy. My foot a canvas, wrapped in canvas. To become potential.

I lace the shoes, step outside where the daybreak
cracks and fires.

At the edge of the pond, my swan is waiting, wings spread. I mount, shoes first. White on white.

In the trees, my camera crews are poised to catch, upload my triumph.

Bedecked in youth's fashion, in beauty, I ride.

APOCRYPHA

Again, we turn to a reading from The Book of Sarah, Chapter 4, Verses 1 through 3.

YET IN a translation of a translation, was whole made hole. For in this translation, Hagar birthed mutating, mutant, and mutated forms, winking and winged, chirruping and flailing in the dark. For her offspring flared up senseless and stunning, and shit silk. For they spasmed, proliferated, flamed and flung. For they exalted the moment through goo and glow.

2 AND THEY spoke great swelling words of vanity, allured through lusts of the flesh. Would hold seven stars in their right hands, and walk in the midst of

seven golden candlesticks. Saw great white thrones, and the queens who sat on them, from whose faces their guts fled.

3 AND SUDDENLY there came a sound like a mighty rushing wind, and it filled the entire house where they were dancing. And divided tongues as of fire appeared to them, and rested on each one of them. And they were each filled with the void, and began to speak in other tongues as the void gave them utterance. For the thrill of the void would give shapeless to their daze.

The
Phantom
Voice

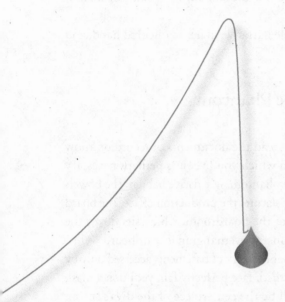

The Diva

Household and empire converge in The Diva's oratory. *Her* household?—picture a penthouse, profanities cast in gold. New money never had it so gaudy, or good. You have seen this diva on television, heard her on the radio, or waited in the crowd, baited and breathless. Have admired the tracks of her flatiron, her iron will, or golden legs.

> *Every man knows her name. Every woman knows her face.*
> *When she walks into a room, all eyes are on Her.*

She is the daughter or the mother or the mouthpiece of a tyrant. In her wake, the bodies are bagged. But her voice—O, to possess such a voice as hers!

> *When she sings—grown men quake, collapse to their knees.*

But this voice is beyond just speech or song. Because—*Hers* is a

21st century voice, it does more than speak up or out. It's the platform itself, control over media and message.

Having His (the Tyrant's) *ear, she's the one who could stop all this, but won't.*

As if she holds the whole narrative in her manicured hand, and bends and bends.

The Phantom

For those of you who do not read the documents of record or know anything about this world in which you live, it is perhaps necessary to introduce myself. *I* am the phantom. My native habitat; the bowels of power. Beneath all, the legislature, the production office, the board room—or the simulacrum of the boardroom, which sits down the hall from the office, with cameras overhanging its cardboard walls.

To find me, follow the subnetwork of basements accessed only by rowboat. My skin is unblemished, face perfectly fair, yet I don a mask *for flair.* This mask that will be the centerpiece of the diva's spring collection, for which I have produced all the most notable designs.

The Diva is my pupil; I her angel of music, by which I mean angel of *rhetoric*, her speechwriter and architect, her maestro of *spin.* I march behind her, she sings *my* happy tune. It is *I* who mold *her.* Characters like *her* will go down in history. Characters like me . . . *create* the history. *I rule* this world so that the Diva and *he*, the Tyrant, may *own* it.

I tell her:

Square your shoulders. Imagine you're a chimney. Your voice hot air, rising from your diaphragm, through the roof. Emptying. Mouth each note just so.

She sings: *Some of my best friends / Are boys / Touching other boys. . . .*

I shout—*Bravissimo!*

Some of my best friends / Are girls / Want equal pay for equal work. . . . Some of my best friends / Are. . . .

On Sunday afternoons, after a long week of tutelage, I huddle under covers, propped by pillows. While the Others, the threatened, take to the square to rally—my shades are drawn.

The Loss / The Lack

Like the Diva, *I too* once had a golden voice. I toured the country in a professional boys' choir. My solos summoned something pure, the Promise of the Nation, under God, guided by angels. I resembled an angel, in my white satin robe, cheeks rouged by a natural, boyish blush. Yet I felt time's noose around my neck, the inevitable loss of this voice I had come to treasure, my sense of self. I saw it coming—a kind of exile.

And then one night I took my position onstage, opened my mouth, and out came a croak. Like something fetid from the bowels of me, rank with age and sex and shame.

Let me be clear: *I* am not the hero, but the *villain* of this story. I was made to ensure *The Legacy of This World's Divas and Tyrants* for generations to come. I am backbone, I am stones. But I'll never be in the history books. My name will never be on an airport or a doctrine. (*In this iteration I am fairly short, not so pretty, and thoroughly homosexual.*) Being the gears behind the voice is as far as my engine goes.

I tell the diva, *I am a monster. But I'm your monster.* And one day, she too will have her platform stolen. Perhaps when she least expects it, perhaps by the upstart she least suspects. Such is the curse of the soprano—whether the Diva, or the phantom who was once a boy.

The Threatened

There *are* others. The threatened. I only mention *them* because you ask.

They are threatened. They are incarcerated. They are waiting in line to file their paperwork. They are evicted. They are Black and brown. They are black and blue. They are targeted. They are warehoused. They are searched. They are raided, then they are fired. They are rehired for less pay by the service hired by the service hired by the same boss who fired them. Some of *them* are resisting. Many resisted long before this tyrant and this diva's reign. On Sundays, they rally in the square.

Others are of little concern to me. *My* concern is taking back what *I've* lost. I douse myself with the Diva's perfume, its bottle emblazoned with the word <i>Complicit</i>.

The Contraption

Being a phantom, I am an architect, an inventor, and an engineer. I am building a contraption.

Its epicenter is an upright stretcher backed by an identical stretcher, framed by an immense decorative armature resembling the pipes of an antique organ. Extending from the stretcher, a tangle of tubes and a cable, which soar toward the ceiling, tethered to an ornate chandelier. And alongside the cable, a trough descending from the ceiling to the stretcher's peak.

The Diva is always my victim. I will strap us into the adjoining stretchers. I will pull a lever and loose the chandelier, which will plummet down the cable, crash, puncture into her body a lattice of holes, through which will worm the tubes. They will siphon fluid, gas, her essence. As her mouth opens wide, her song transforms into a scream, molten gold from the walls of her penthouse will ooze from the trough down her throat, fill her lungs and gut. But it's the steam that will kill her, upon which she'll choke.

She arrives for her daily lesson, sees my contraption.

I didn't realize you had such a kinky side—Some of my best friends are freaks. . . .

This is not an assassination—*Her* death is but a byproduct. I simply aim to steal her voice.

The Execution

The Diva writhes and screams, *Why are you doing this? Please let me go!*

Without me to script her, such lackluster speech.

I ask her, *Is it possible that you've confused me with the tyrant and his followers—that gang of backward children you play tricks on?*

That I should want her voice at all suddenly strikes me as the height of improbability. But the Diva is an improbable character, and so am *I*—insatiable, ambitious, unable to love or be loved.

Through the tubes that connect us, her power courses. I throb and pulse. Feel the architecture of my platform taking shape. I can already see them, those women and men who adore her, falling at my feet. They cry, Make me great again! And so I will.

The Reckoning

And so—will I?

Here is a joke: How many *cis*gays does it take to build an empire?

Here is a riddle: Outside the basement, where is the ceiling, the limits of subversion?

In the square, the threatened are gathered.

Even in the Tyrant's America, I could choose to relinquish my platform.

I could.

Here is an inquiry: Will my faggotry ever be more than whiteness, wit and spectacle? State your answer in the form of a question. What is a high note. What is shattered glass.

APOCRYPHA

II

Chapter 5,
Verse 1

5 AND THE creature
Sarah unfolded
their two great wings, and
soared to their place in the
wilderness, where they planted
a prayer for our next (their
own) translation, the one called
liberation, where my evil gives
way to _____ .

Notes
&
Acknowledgments

Notes:

Small portions of "Cathedral Ceilings" borrow and torque, and / or recontextualize language from Raymond Carver's "Cathedral," as well as the article, "The Long Delayed Success of Frank Grillo," from *Backstage Magazine*.

Its concept was inspired by Kevin Killian's story, "White Rose," a homoerotic reinterpretation of Flannery O'Connor's "A Good Man is Hard to Find."

"Figures Up Ahead, Moving in the Trees" appropriates language from the song "These Dreams," by Heart.

"We Are Going to Wilmington, North Carolina!" appropriates plot elements and smatterings of dialogue from the television series *Dawson's Creek* and *One Tree Hill*, and borrows /adapts lyrics from songs used on the former series, including those performed by Paula Cole, Chantal Kreviazuk and Heather Nova.

"Teenagers' Need" were crafted via an adapted take on Dodie Bellamy's "cunt up" method, combined with a meme described by Matias Viegener in *2500 Random Things About Me Too*.

"Meet #AlexFromTarget: An American Boy," is patterned after the book *Meet Samantha: An American Girl*," by Susan S. Adler.

"Limelight Memories" is informed by the narratives of sexual assault survivors from Horace Mann School, and in particular, the essay "The Master," by Marc Fisher, appearing in *The New Yorker*. It borrows

163

dialogue from the films
All About Eve, Mildred Pierce, Mommie Dearest and *Showgirls.*
"Apocrypha" appropriates language from Joyelle McSweeney's essay, "Bug Time: Chitinous Necropastoral Hypertime Against the Future."

"The Phantom Voice" was sparked by my reading of several interviews with the author Alexander Chee, in which he discusses the trauma of losing his boyhood soprano voice while part of a professional boys' choir.

It appropriates, and in most cases transforms or otherwise torques, language and/or other elements from Gaston Leroux's *Phantom of the Opera;* Wayne Koestenbaum's *The Queen's Throat: Opera,* *Homosexuality, and the Mystery of Desire;* the film *All About Eve; Saturday Night Live's* mock perfume ad for "Complicit"; and the television series *Scandal.*

Acknowledgments

Stories from this collection appeared in the following publications, some in different forms:

"Tim Jones-Yelvington is a Pretty Little Liar" in *Red Lightbulbs* and *Become On Yr Face* (New Michigan Press)

"Old Testament," "New Testament," "The Gospel," "Apocrypha" and "Apocrypha (2)" in *The Account,* as "Abraham the Daddy, Isaac the Boy."

"Divine Decree" in *Signal Mountain Review*

"Figures Up Ahead, Moving in the Trees" in *Always Crashing*

"Cathedral Ceilings" in *Bosie*

"We Are Going to Wilmington, North Carolina!" in *New South*

"Teenagers' Need" in *Fanzine*

"Meet #AlexFromTarget, An American Boy" in *Grimoire*

"Limelight Memories" in *SPECS*

"Daniel, Damned," as a limited-edition chapbook from Solar Luxuriance Press

"The Phantom Voice" in *Yes Femmes*